The Enchanted Lands of

Norway

Barents Sea

Stabbursdalen National Park

Seiland

Varanger Peninsula

Vadsø

Jerndor

Thief of Peace's Passage

Tromsø

Niflheim

Jotunheim

Lord Well

Norwegian Sea

Malmdor

The Neighboring Kingdom of Sweden

Ellehen

Glade of the Golden Rings

Allheim

Trondheim

Gjallarbrú

Kristiansund

Trolgar

Bergen

Mountains

Oslo

Fredrikstad

Stavanger

Skagerrak Strait

North Sea

The Kingdom of Denmark

A Zaria Fierce Novel

Aleks Mickelsen and the Eighth Fox Throne War

By Keira Gillett

E-book ISBN: 978-1-942750-12-3

Paperback ISBN: 978-1-942750-11-6

LCCN: 2019902110

Special Offer: You can snatch book two for free when you sign up for Keira Gillett's mailing list. Grab your copy of *Zaria Fierce and the Enchanted Drakeland Sword* in the e-book format of your choice.

Join Team Fierce Today:

https://www.keiragillett.com/free-download/

Reading Order:

Zaria Fierce and the Secret of Gloomwood Forest

Zaria Fierce and the Enchanted Drakeland Sword

Zaria Fierce and the Dragon Keeper's Golden Shoes

Aleks Mickelsen and the Twice-Lost Fairy Well

Aleks Mickelsen and the Call of the White Raven

Aleks Mickelsen and the Eighth Fox Throne War

Praise for Zaria Fierce and the Secret of Gloomwood Forest

"Are you in the mood for an old fashioned magical jaunt? Zaria Fierce and the Secret of Gloomwood Forest by Keira Gillett is a classic "perilous adventure" book for middle grade readers." *Jennifer Bardsley, The YA Gal*

"A captivating blending of fantasy storytelling with today's technology. At the base of this tale is deep, abiding friendship that stands the tests of time, adventure and even danger." *Kathy Haw, Goodreads Review*

"If you're looking for an action-packed adventure dipped in fantasy, look no further. This book kept me on my toes with its many cliffhangers and plot twists; it was quite hard to put down at times." *Meredith, All 'Bout Them Books and Stuff*

"This was a really good book with a great setting and cool plot line. I really liked how it didn't hide that Zaria was adopted and she knew it. I also liked how her adoptive parents were nice. You don't see that often in books (as an adopted kid, I like it when adoption is portrayed well)." *Erik, This Kid Reviews Books*

"A great book with vivid descriptions and relatable characters. The main character becomes a strong female lead, and the writing and illustrations make this fantasy world even more real and interesting." *Analee, Book Snacks*

Praise for Zaria Fierce and the Enchanted Drakeland Sword

"The Zaria Fierce series just keeps getting better, with this sequel! This is an awesome fantasy filled with suspense, from the first page to the last! The vivid descriptions combined with the beautiful illustrations make the setting come to life." *Brandi Nyborg, Goodreads Review*

"This is one of the most amazing second books in a trilogy that I've read. I like how empowering the book is, especially on facing your own demons. Just like Zaria." *Danissa, The Booklandia*

"I like how the action begins quickly and Gillett brings the reader up to speed on the plot, no time is wasted in getting these friends off on another adventure through the Norwegian countryside. Oh, and that setting, it's one of the most enjoyable things in reading Gillett's stories. All the lovely rich details of each of the magical kingdoms, each place is unique and highlights the depth of her imagination." *Brenda, Log Cabin Library*

"Zaria is both vulnerable and strong, and very much a role model for my own daughters." *APinFL, Audible Review*

Praise for Zaria Fierce and the Dragon Keeper's Golden Shoes

"The Zaria Fierce trilogy is a fun middle grade adventure with a great message, and *Zaria Fierce and the Dragon Keeper's Golden Shoes* rounds it out perfectly! Zaria and her friends are realistic characters and I thoroughly appreciated the exploration of their friendship and growth as individuals and as a group. I think the Zaria Fierce series deserves a lot more love!" *Nicole, Read Eat Sleep Repeat*

"*Zaria Fierce and the Dragon Keeper's Golden Shoes* was the magical conclusion this trilogy asked for. Filled with action and adventure, Zaria and her friends showed us the importance of teamwork, friendship, and having courage in ourselves. The perfect ending to a fun series, I recommend this to all fantasy lovers, middle school and beyond!" *Emily, Midwestern Book Nerd*

"*Zaria Fierce and the Dragon Keeper's Golden Shoes* was a spectacular conclusion to a great trilogy (though the ending left the door open for more adventures). Filled with magic, a great story line, amazing and real characters, wonderful settings and beautifully explored themes, Keira Gillett created a trilogy that I will always cherish and will visit anytime. If you like The Chronicles of Narnia, *The Hobbit,* The Spiderwick Chronicles or simply love a book filled with Norwegian folklore and fantasy, then this is the ultimate series for you to read, devour and lose yourselves in." *Ner, A Cup of Coffee and a Book*

Praise for Aleks Mickelsen and the Twice-Lost Fairy Well

"You don't realise how much you miss things till they are gone, and this is the case with this series. The characters had a way of worming themselves into my heart and I missed them! Well, they are back and better than ever!!" *Natalie, Book Lover's Life*

"I loved the first three Zaria books and I have to say I'm even more in love with Aleks! I was surprised by the many twists and turns of the book and loved catching up with all the new and old characters. This book would be a great gift for any young teenager and it's a great read for an adult like myself." *Rusty Forsmark, Amazon Review*

"There is so much that I loved about this story. Aleks is one of my favorite characters and I am so excited that he is getting his own stories so that readers can learn more about him and go on this journey of self-discovery along with him and his friends." *Bridgett, Little Bee's Reads*

"I must find a way to sneak a stargazer along with a thousand pesky request letters in the mail to the author to try to get the next book to come out faster!" *Ronald Shaw, Audible Review*

Praise for Aleks Mickelsen and the Call of the White Raven

"This volume of the Zaria Fierce series feels like a fun camping trip. A combination of an adventure and a love story. Entertaining from beginning to end and recommended." *Christian, Audible Review*

"Everything you love about the Zaria Fierce books is here: the strong friendships, the nonstop adventure, the magical creatures, and the hero's quest are all here, waiting for fantasy lovers to join them. Keira Gillett's at the height of her storytelling here;" *Rosemary, Mom Read It*

"I really enjoyed this next book. Aleks is definitely becoming my favorite character in the series. Seeing him face his fear, and his fate, in accepting who he is, has made me think, and reminds me of my own individual quest for identity." *Daniel, Audible Review*

Praise for Aleks Mickelsen and the Eighth Fox Throne War

"From the opening sentence of the prologue to the final paragraph, you know you are in a fierce adventure. Having been with the series since the beginning, it has been wonderful following our group through all the action! *Aleks Mickelsen and the Eighth Fox Throne War* abounds with magic and if fey politics don't get you killed, the dragon just might ... or a beautiful fairy's father... Settle in and get ready for a great story from one of my favorite authors." *Tammy Spencer, Goodreads Review*

"I held my breath many times reading this book. The challenges are nonstop. You'll find plenty of fierce battles and extremely scary creatures. But, as always in this series, friendship, cooperation, and just the right amount of humor offer hope in the darkest of times." *Patricia Mather Parker, Author of The Abode*

"Keira does it again in the third Aleks Mickelsen book! Full of adventure, the story continues on as the gang tries to fool the plans of Fritjof, a dragon that is sneakier than a snake. Keira's writing always impresses me... A highly enjoyable read for all ages!" *Amanda, Goodreads Review*

Dedication:

I dedicate this book to Karen Brown, my talented and amazing editor. You truly make the writing shine and are an asset to the series. I couldn't do this without you. Thank you for being my friend and supporting me throughout this project.

Special Thanks:

Thanks for to these individuals for their input on the book cover: Michele Carpenter, Gus Boniface, Shawn Meyer, and Karin Gillett. I'm truly warmed by it.

To Readers:

I am so glad you're here as we embark together on a new and exciting chapter in Aleks' trilogy. Before we get started, I wanted to share a little background on a word you will find in this book: Firething is a combination of two words – 'fire,' the Norwegian word for four and 'thing', the Norwegian word for assembly. It is pronounced like fee-rah instead of the English word fire. Thing is still pronounced as thing in this spelling. If you forget, fire thing still sounds pretty cool! Are you ready? Hang on to your feathers and tails, we're about to run headfirst into danger.

Table of Contents

Illustrations

Prologue: Doomed from the Start

"Ah!" shrieked a startled Christoffer, stumbling backwards from the passage, his black hair falling into brown eyes. "I didn't mean it!"

Of course, *of course*, Christoffer would tempt fate, Aleks thought, as he stared in horror at the neon yellow eyes gleaming menacingly in the dark. While his blithe-spirited friend lacked impulse control, Aleks couldn't blame Christoffer for the dragon's appearance. He would have appeared regardless. But still, did he have to ask for trouble?

"Watch out," shouted Airi, Aleks' white raven, taking flight in fright.

"Too late," muttered his best friend, Geirr, crouching as the door swung open on creaky hinges.

The Thief of Peace's Passage, an underground corridor between the fey realm and the dwarf kingdom, opened at midnight and closed at dawn every day without fail. Nothing Christoffer did, or didn't do, would have changed that, but why, why did he have to knock and ask if anybody was on the other side of the door? Of all the brainless things to ask.

Because there was someone—thing waiting for them. The echoes of Fritjof's sinister words rang in his ears. He'd been waiting for them, for this moment. Sweat broke out along his brow, and his mouth went drier than the Gobi Desert. They were unprepared. They weren't ready. They were doomed.

Fritjof, the dragon of chaos, was the youngest of the three original dragons to come into the world. Aleks and his friends had first come across Fritjof when his eldest brother, Koll, the dragon of darkness, had been slain by Aleks' friend, Zaria Fierce, a sorceress princess and daughter of Queen Helena, Dragon Keeper of the Under Realm – a prison for dragons.

Because Zaria possessed a rare type of magic controlled by thought alone, she was able to do what no others had ever done before. It was crucial therefore that dragons not learn the nature of her powers as they would have torn her limb from limb as they had done to the last young sorceress to possess thought magic.

To protect her, Helena had given Zaria up for adoption to the Fierce's, who knew nothing of her magical powers, when she was a baby. Mother and daughter had recently reconnected because of the machinations of Koll and a hapless river-troll named Olaf, who'd been manipulated by the dragon. When Koll figured out the truth behind Zaria's powers, he'd whisked her away to a final battle of wills and magic; one that she had won.

Left behind to face a different battle, Aleks and his friends had squared off against the remaining dragon brother... no, *brothers*. At least that's what Aleks thought had happened. When Nori, his fey sibling, had arrived to warn him Fritjof was trying to escape, he hadn't believed her. After all, he wouldn't forget battling a dragon, right? *Wrong.*

In the midst of the battle, Fritjof had slipped away unnoticed. He'd then erased all memories of his existence from the minds of everyone, including his sympathizers and his enemies. Even Aleks and his friends hadn't remembered him, and it didn't seem to matter that they knew they should. Aleks couldn't even remember him now, despite staring into Fritjof's evil face.

Only Nori, with her gift of knowing the truth, had remembered Fritjof. She had seen the signs of his presence in Niffleheim, the realm of the fairies—and their current location. She had first tried to warn her fey family; but Grimkell, their father, and the ruler of the Autumn Court in Niffleheim, hadn't acted and had been overthrown by his sister, Cornelia, and her husband, Ytorm.

Knowing she wouldn't gain the support she needed from her aunt and uncle to stop Fritjof, Nori had sought help outside the realm. She'd gone to Aleks and his friends. That's how they had ended up here facing down Fritjof, about to be dragon kibble.

Oh, there'd been stuff in between Nori's appearance at his bedroom window in Fredrikstad and this moment, of course. They'd encountered power-hungry mountain trolls and rescued imprisoned troll children. Aleks had bonded with a white raven that could talk and gone through a series of cruel trials starting in a dark, dank, oubliette that would've broken the spirit of a lesser person and nearly had broken him.

Aleks was a changeling, despised by his fey family who would kill him on the spot. He was losing his fey powers as he grew more human and would lose all his magic at age sixteen if he chose to stay with his adoptive human family. Losing his pointy ears, which set him apart from his friends, had been one of the biggest perks of his upcoming birthday only eight days away.

Now it seemed his choice to live as a human had been taken from him. The Lost Well had a different path for him, and in bonding to him had brought back his fey powers. Aleks regained the ability to shapeshift into a fox, something a changeling shouldn't be able to do. Worst of all, with the return of his powers, his ears, which had become less pointy over the years spent with his human family, had returned with a vengeance. He would now be doomed to sport them all his life.

All these happenings had been unwelcomed signs that the witch of the woods' prediction that he'd ascend to the throne was coming true. Nori had tried to claim the throne with a wish; Grimkell had tried to help him with the trials in order to get him out of Niffleheim faster; and his aunt and uncle had tried to turn him and his friends into runts – slaves – in order to augment their claim to rule.

In the end, it hadn't mattered that he or many in his fey family didn't want him to stay in Niffleheim, let alone be king. Upon conclusion of the trials, word had spread far and wide in the Autumn Court, and many fey had come to witness his triumph.

A king or queen of Niffleheim was distinguished from a ruler, because instead of reigning over a single court, the monarch ruled over all four courts. Aleks had been declared the former, much to Grimkell's displeasure, though his birth father's displeasure paled in comparison to Aleks' own.

He had been depending on turning human when he reached his majority. He'd been so close. But how could the king of Niffleheim turn human? It would never happen. Maybe he would've chosen to stay a changeling. Then again, maybe not. That was the crux of the problem. He hadn't had a choice.

But all this misfortune faded in comparison to the worst trial of them all – Fritjof present, here and now. And even though Aleks already had seen signs of the dragon's presence, it wasn't until this moment that all doubt left him. He had hoped Nori was wrong, but the pair of glowing yellow eyes before him was proof of her assertion that Fritjof existed. There was no escape. No plan. No hope. Aleks felt panicked and alone.

"Not alone," cried Airi, his white raven, circling overhead.

Had she somehow read his thoughts? Had he spoken aloud? Or was she simply referring to the dragon lurking nearby? Airi was highly intelligent and he didn't yet know all that she was capable of. Stranger things had happened, but Aleks couldn't focus in order to find out.

Beside him, Zaria leapt to her feet, raising her hands defensively. "Stay back!" she shouted at the dragon.

"Stay back," mocked Fritjof. "Oh, I think not, Princess. Why don't you come into my lair? Save your little friends while you can."

"I'm not afraid of you," she said, purple magic glowing between her hands. She shot the fireball at the dragon, straight between his eyes.

"Yeah," cried Christoffer, pumping a fist in the air. "Go Zaria! Team Fierce all the way!"

The fireball sailed harmlessly through its target, exploding inside the tunnel. The burst of light revealed an empty passageway. As the light faded, the pair of glowing eyes returned. They blazed in wicked amusement.

"Didn't you children know you were doomed from the start?" Fritjof asked mildly. "There's nothing you can do to stop me. I've already won."

"Not yet, you haven't!" shouted Zaria, gearing up for another fireball.

"Your magic can't harm me," Fritjof jeered, sending forth a blast of wind.

The fireball snuffed out. His hissing laugh slithered down Aleks' spine like phantom fingers, spurring him to action. In one fluid movement, Aleks plucked his bow off the ground, grabbed a single arrow from his quiver, and stood tall.

"We have more than magic on our side," he said, taking aim.

Fritjof's eyes narrowed. "What makes you think your pathetic little arrow can do any better?"

Aleks hesitated, his grip slacking on the bowstring. He didn't know if the arrow would work. Why would it, if Zaria's magic couldn't harm him? The wave of panic returned, coupled with confusion, immobilizing him. He didn't know what to do.

"What are you waiting for, Aleks? Shoot him!" shouted Geirr, leaping to his feet, daggers in hand, his preferred weapon.

The skinny, well-dressed teen bravely faced off against Fritjof, brandishing his blades, a sight which woke up Aleks. Shaking away the miasma overriding his thoughts, Aleks pulled the arrow back, drawing the string taut.

"I wouldn't do that if I were you," taunted Fritjof. "You'll regret it most severely if you do."

"Don't listen to him," said Christoffer. "He's just scared. Fire!"

He released his breath, focused down his arm, and let the arrow go. It whizzed through the air in a straight trajectory... right between the dragon's eyes. His heart sank; the arrow had disappeared in the dark, only to land with a sharp metallic *thwack*.

Fritjof's glowing yellow eyes returned, dancing in the dark. "You're in trouble now," he said with another of his hissing laughs.

Chapter One: At Least It's Not the Wild Hunt

"What did your arrow hit?" asked Filip, warily getting to his feet. Green eyes squinting, he tried to peer through the blue-black darkness into the heart of the tunnel. "Zar-Zar, can you let loose another fireball?"

"No problem," she said and shot off another purple ball of flame.

Like the arrow and fireball before them, the new attack sailed through the dragon's floating, mocking eyes. It exploded against the wall, showering the tunnel in light, revealing the unintended target of Aleks' shot. An armored dwarf with braided hair the color of wheat stood a short distance inside, shielding her eyes from the unexpected light.

She lowered her gaze to her other arm, which bore a strapped wooden and metallic shield. Lodged in its center was Aleks' arrow. The dwarf grabbed the shaft and yanked it out, examining the pointed tip with an angry grimace, pulling her eyebrows inward to meet the bridge of her nose.

Slowly standing, Henrik held out both hands in supplication. The dwarf stared at him suspiciously, taking in his golden-antlered white cloak and pale brown hair. "Don't be alarmed," he said in a soft, soothing voice. "We meant no harm."

"I find that hard to believe, Stag Lord," she said, snapping the arrow in half, and dropping the pieces unceremoniously to the floor.

"It's true. We didn't see you there," said Zaria. "I'm going to toss another fireball for light; is that okay?"

At the dwarf's nod, she lobbed a purple fireball, careful to aim high to avoid the irate dwarf.

"Why were you standing there in the dark?" asked Geirr, running a hand over his close-cropped black hair. "One doesn't just simply stand around in the Thief of Peace's Passage. That's pretty dodgy."

"I came to scout the source of the purple light," she said witheringly. "You're not in need of help."

"We do need help," said Aleks, earnestly. "There's a dragon trying to escape from the passage."

"Liar," she spat, crushing the arrow beneath her heel. "I've been in the passage for days. There's nothing here, except unruly fairies and their *little* friends."

"She's one to talk," said Christoffer under his breath, wincing as Henrik elbowed him hard.

"What is your name?" asked Zaria.

The dwarf glowered, her hazel eyes narrowing as if looking for a trick. "I'm Frigga."

She smiled and touched her collarbone. "Nice to meet you, Frigga. I'm Princess Zar–"

"I know who you are," she sneered, showing teeth. "There aren't that many sorceresses."

Filip gestured at the tunnel. "His name is Fritjof. The dragon, I mean. We saw him there, which is why Aleks shot–"

"I'll hear no more of your lies," Frigga said, stopping him. "Floki was right about you, about everything."

"What are you talking about?" asked Aleks.

"He said you framed him, to keep him from revealing the truth – that you'd stop at nothing to remake the realms in your image."

Aleks scoffed, "Frame him? Why would we do that? We didn't even know of him before that narcissistic weasel aided a dragon so he could overthrow your King Flein, – his own father. You can't trust anything he says."

"The rest of his accusation is also ridiculous," Geirr added. "We don't seek to change anybody's realms."

"He said you'd say that," she muttered to herself.

"Because he knows he's lying," Christoffer said.

She continued as if she didn't hear them. "He even said you'd go so far as to conjure up stories about dragons to get people to do what you wanted without questioning it. I had some doubts, but this just proves it. There's no dragon here."

"There was," Zaria insisted. "Please believe us. Floki lied to you. There are dragons trying to escape my mother's realm."

Frigga hesitated, looking at each of them in turn. Then a strange light gleamed in her eyes as she looked down and saw the broken arrow. Raising her gaze, she hissed, "You'll rue this day when you attacked the great kingdom of Jerndor."

"Wait," said Zaria desperately, stepping forward with a pleading hand outstretched. "We're all on the same side."

"Never," she said, before turning and running down the tunnel, shouting at the top of her lungs, "We're under attack! We're under attack! Princess Zaria and the Stag Lord attacked!"

Henrik cursed. "That's not true," he shouted at the dwarf's retreating form.

"It was a mistake," cried Zaria. "We didn't mean to attack you at all!"

Geirr arched an eyebrow. "What's all the fuss about, anyhow? It was one measly arrow. It didn't even do any damage."

The purple glow faded and in the shifting dark Fritjof's mocking eyes twinkled merrily like an evil Cheshire Cat. "You'd best run, children. There's a dwarf army on its way," he said.

"You did this," Zaria accused. "I don't know how, but you're why she was in the tunnel and why the arrow hit her."

"And if I did arrange it as you say, Princess? What are you going to do about it?" Fritjof asked.

"Stop you," crowed Airi, landing on Aleks' shoulder and gripping tight. He felt the words echo in his heart, strengthening him. Together they'd taken on one dragon and won. They could do it again.

"You can try," Fritjof said, before blinking and disappearing. One second a pair of floating eyes shone as bright as headlamps, the next, darkness enshrouded everything.

A war cry blasted from the tunnel, blowing back Aleks' hair. It rivaled any call from the Wild Hunt. Who knew that beings so small could raise terror like that? They had to get out of here. There was no time to waste.

Lunging for his stuff, Aleks tossed Christoffer's bag to him, while the others copied, picking up as much of their camp as they could, including lanterns to light their way.

An axe hurtled through the open door, landing in the dirt just before Aleks' feet. He looked up, holding his stargazer aloft. His gut tightened in trepidation, relaxing slightly as a single broad-chested dwarf exited the passage.

"Halt!" she cried, whether to them or the soldiers in the passage, Aleks had no idea.

"Who are you?" asked Zaria, hands loose at her sides, her anxiety hidden, except for the purple magic sparking at her fingertips.

"Brunhild, Lieutenant of the Ravagers, and you are the spoiled princess who attacked my scout. What was it? A perverse sort of tantrum?"

"No!" cried Zaria.

Brunhild looked at them, and they at her. She wore fitted iron battle armor – a good choice when facing fairies, who were susceptible to the metal. It covered her from wrist to ankles, and didn't expose an inch of skin. It was clear she was an officer; clipped to her side was a beautifully finished steel sword with a huge emerald embedded in its hilt. Her open-faced helmet had a nose-guard, and was as ornate as her sword. Sprouting from the top crest, waved a single large white plume.

Shifting movement behind her drew Aleks' attention. His eyes widened in alarm. "Run!" he shouted, slinging his bag over his shoulder.

"Get them!" Brunhild bellowed, and a troop of female warriors in fitted breastplates poured out of the passage like ants spilling out from a kicked over anthill.

Aleks and his friends ran as if their lives depended on it – and they definitely did – racing up a short staircase and farther up a steep incline, retracing their way back toward the heart of Niffleheim. Zaria threw out wild bolts of energy, trying to keep the Ravagers back without harming them. When the dwarven regiment realized she wasn't aiming to kill, and barely aiming to wound, they charged.

Filip grabbed her, forcing her to stop tossing magic and run flat out. The dwarves pursued, their armor clanking at the joints. It sounded like a hundred brass cymbals smashing together simultaneously, at once both deafening and jarring in the echoing spaces of the underground void.

"How did we not hear them in the tunnels?" asked Henrik, chancing a look behind them.

Christoffer ran, covering his ears. "They're enough to wake the dead," he said.

"It was Fritjof!" Aleks shouted to be heard over the din. "He somehow blocked their noise."

"I really hate dragons, *especially* this guy," wheezed Geirr, slowing down and grabbing his side. "First he crashes my plane, and then he sends an army after us. So uncool, man."

Aleks grabbed his friend's arm and propelled him upward, feeling his blood pumping. "Don't stop. Keep running. We're almost to the plains."

The plains was a nearly featureless area, which lay below the main living region of Niffleheim. It connected the four courts on a subterranean level, making it an ideal place to launch an invasion against one of the other courts. For this reason, it had to be guarded against and Aleks hoped it was equally guarded against rampaging dwarves.

The Thief of Peace's Passage, which led to the dwarves, and the Lost Well (also found on the same level as the plains) were the only connections to the real world. The well was a source of tremendous power for the fey. All four courts sought the Lost Well in order to claim it and the Great Fox Throne.

The one who ruled the well, ruled over all. The other courts would be forced to swear fealty or lose all access to it. Each court's ruling nobles feared that the well's power would end up in the hands of their nemesis, hence the many countless patrols and surveys made over hundreds of years in hopes of discovering its location.

But the magic cast by Zaria's mother, Queen Helena, after the signing of the Dragomir Treaty, obscured it from them. It had been deemed dangerous by the rest of the magical community for the fey to hold on to its power. Helena's magic had done its job perfectly, and no fey had been successful in finding it or claiming the Lost Well for nearly a thousand years. Aleks, however, had been destined to find it and unwittingly bonded with the well when recovering his stargazer, dropped into its depths by his white raven.

Looking at her now, gliding above him, Aleks called out, "Fly ahead and warn my sister. We're going to need backup!"

She peeled off, crying, "Eye-riii! Eye-riii!"

One by one Aleks and his friends splashed through a creek that bisected the incline, forming a small plateau before sharply rising again. Wading through the mud, Aleks made a mental note to destroy his shoes at the first opportunity. They were already heavily encrusted from the trials, and now this new mud was like carrying an extra five pounds on each foot. He felt his energies begin to flag.

The dwarvish soldiers pursued them up the incline, their stomping feet almost perfectly in unison with their neighbors. Some beat their breastplates, adding to the cacophony. Clang. Clang. Clang. The sound rattled off the walls and reverberated like death knells in Aleks' ears.

He groaned and huffed, unable to keep pushing Geirr uphill. The others tired quickly, too. Still, they persisted, forcing one foot in front of the other. It didn't make a difference. Every time Aleks looked back, it appeared that the dwarves steadily gained on them. If he and his friends didn't get to the top fast enough, the plains would be their last stand.

Emerging from the bowels of the fey realm, Aleks led the way to the Autumn Court. It was probably unnecessary at this point to take the lead, but as the group's navigator, it was an ingrained habit. They hadn't made it very far into the plains, when spears with sharp, narrow heads thunked point down in the ground all around them, trapping them in a circle.

"We have to keep creating distance," Henrik said, grabbing a spear from beside him and lobbing it back.

The dwarves raised round wooden shields, deflecting the attack. As more joined them, the women spread out, spears and axes ready in hand.

"We're sitting ducks," Zaria shouted, zapping a hooked spear away from her. It disappeared into thin air, arriving where, Aleks knew not.

A set of spears – one barbed, one hooked – shot toward her. She did the same to them as she had the first spear, and retaliated by tossing a fireball at the brigade. They ducked, throwing up their shields, but Zaria once again purposefully aimed high to avoid hurting their foes. She and Aleks did not want a war on their hands. They were trying to diffuse one.

"We have to snuff our lanterns. It's the only way!" cried Filip. "Turn off your stargazer, Aleks."

He did, clicking a button within a star cutout on the egg-shaped device. His friends likewise darkened their lanterns, deliberately shattering them against the ground. After a brief flare of light as oil and fuel burned bright, the world went dark, and Aleks had to clear spots from his vision.

It was still night, sometime past midnight, and all was pitch black. The scalloped icy ceiling over the plains offered no hint of recourse. In an instant the tide had turned, and their attackers were on the defensive. The all-female dwarf unit came to a stumbling, crashing halt.

Aleks couldn't see it, but he pictured the scene like one of the cartoons he had watched growing up, with one soldier running into another and causing a chain reaction, sending everyone toppling like dominos.

Dwarves shouted and groaned, hurling insults at one another like they hurled spears. Some hit their marks with deadly accuracy, as barbed as some of the real spears lobbed in their direction. Wounded egos and pride ripped through the troop, tumbling them into chaos.

The Ravagers had relied on the light generated by Aleks and the others to direct their attacks. Without it, the soldiers were as blinded by the darkness as Aleks and his friends. Try as they might, none of the female warriors could move for knocking into someone or tripping over the uneven ground. Unlike the dwarves, however, they stayed quiet, essentially becoming invisible to any straining ears close by.

Zaria touched his sleeve, making him jump. "Easy," she whispered, leaning close. "Do you think you can lead us in the dark?"

Aleks' fairy power was the ability to navigate on instinct. He always knew where he was going… well, he used to know. Lately, his magic wasn't always right at hand, and he'd unwittingly taken his friends down many wrong turns and paths; but, they'd always forgiven him, and somehow they'd always ended up right where they were supposed to be. He knew without asking they all had his back.

The inner debate roiled in him. Could he lead them? Glitchy powers or not, Aleks felt certain he could. This was a path he'd taken before, so he had a pretty solid idea of what to expect and where to go. Instead of giving a verbal answer that might give away their position to the nearby dwarves, he took Zaria's small, slender hand in his and tugged her forward in the dark. She understood him, like she always did, and followed without hesitation.

In turn, with equally unspoken communication, she grabbed someone else's hand. They all linked up, and Aleks made confident strides forward, even though he couldn't see the end of his nose. He didn't need his sight to find his way.

His power worked almost like a feeling. Perhaps it would be accurate to describe it as a sixth sense. In his mind he could see the layout of the plains like a map. He knew where they were in relation to their objective – the entrance to the Autumn Court. He also knew how close they were to the sensory onslaught indicating where the dwarves stood next to the plains' entrance to the Thief of Peace's Passage.

He guided his friends over the uneven terrain. The plains were relatively flat, but rolled slightly underfoot. The occasional stalagmite had to be circumnavigated. The further away they got, the more muddled the dwarves sounded. Their racket faded into a dull din.

Aleks used their fixed location to steer his friends through the cavern. It felt good to be leading his friends again, with some semblance of sureness. He hoped his confidence wasn't misplaced. He hoped Zaria's wasn't either.

"Are we there yet?" asked Christoffer from the back of the group.

"Shh," Zaria chided. "Keep your voice down."

Distracted by their whispering, Aleks stumbled, slamming headfirst into a wall. Zaria instantly let go of his hand and scrambled to help him up. Another pair of hands joined in and lifted him.

Wincing, he rubbed the bridge of his nose with one hand and reached out with the other to touch the surface of the cavern wall. The cold, rough stone bit into his flesh. How had he missed that?

"Are you okay, mate?" Filip asked. "You should watch where you're going."

"Ha. Ha. You're hilarious," muttered Aleks, dropping his hands.

Nothing had changed in the last little bit. The cavern was still pitch black. He looked left and right, trying to discern something, to regain his bearings, but the mental map he'd been following had winked out, almost as if it had gotten knocked out of his head when he'd hit the wall. He held back a disgusted sigh.

Light flickered behind him. Turning to look, Aleks saw that the dwarves had finally gotten their act together. Torches were being lit, illuminating pointy chins, strong cheekbones, robust figures, and braided hairstyles. The dwarf women looked ready to skewer. The Ravagers were closing in on them.

"We need to keep going," said Henrik. "We shouldn't look back again. Their lights might reflect in our eyes and give away our position."

Geirr turned, his dim outline facing resolutely forward. "Lead on," he said, waving Aleks ahead.

He hesitated. "I've lost the way," he admitted, scratching his neck and trying not to squirm.

In the dim light, Aleks saw Zaria frown. Concern etched on her face as she reached out to touch his arm. "I don't like that this keeps happening."

"Me neither," said Aleks, looking away to hide his frustration. So what *was* the explanation?

The prevailing theory pointed to dragon interference, which even the Lost Well could not block. The other less likely theory, considering all the facts, hit near the heart. His majority was close at hand. If he became human, he'd be stripped of all powers, including his navigational sixth sense and his more recently acquired ability of shapeshifting. To keep his powers he needed to be as far from his human family as possible on his birthday.

Because he was currently away from his home, his powers should be stabilizing, but they weren't. In fact, they should be growing, since he'd bonded with the Lost Well. He suppressed a mirthless laugh. Only he could find himself in such an untenable paradoxical position. His bond with the well meant he was regaining powers he'd once lost, but it hadn't stopped the slow degradation of his navigational power.

When Aleks, lost in his thoughts, said nothing further, Henrik cleared his throat. "I can lead us," he said, pulling Zaria away, with Filip a step behind, and leading into the darkness ahead.

Aleks followed, thinking hard. He hadn't wanted to be king, but he hadn't been able to refuse once he'd seen the faces of the commoners and the hope in their eyes. They'd registered with him, not as faceless masses, but as people. He knew it wouldn't be so easy to leave it all behind for a normal human life.

He stared at nothing, trying to rebuild the map in his head. He didn't like feeling helpless. Not being able to navigate was like losing a piece of himself. It was a piece he always thought he could live without, but now he wasn't so sure. He had basically a week to decide what to do. That is, if he still had a choice in the matter. Could he go against the well?

From the moment he learned he was a changeling, Aleks had wanted to be human. It wasn't just the pointy ears that he didn't like, although for a long time it had been the biggest reason. His grams had told him many stories about the fey's true nature. Then he had witnessed their conniving and self-serving ways first-hand.

One only needed to look at his birth father, Grimkell, to see a consummate example of what the fey represented as a whole. Grimkell was like a chess player, dealing with people as if they were pieces he could manipulate with a cold-hearted ruthlessness, arranging everyone and everything to his liking. Aleks had no desire to turn into him.

On the other hand, Grimkell wasn't the only example to be had. There was Saskia, a winter fairy with the heart of a warrior and the beauty and vivacity of a songbird. She made him question everything he thought he knew about what it meant to be fey. Currently, she was off with a diplomatic delegation to see her father, the general of the Winter Court. The very thought of seeing her again quickened his pulse.

Then there was his sister, Nori. He'd seen how she could lay her dreams of power aside in order to help him and his friends. He hadn't known before that the fey could be self-sacrificing. She certainly hadn't seemed the type – rude, cold, and snobbish.

Thinking about what she'd done for him twisted his insides. He didn't know how to thank her for her help and support. Because of her, Aleks and his friends had survived a coup d'état on the throne... and she had also led him to become king over the fey. Even if he hadn't wanted it, that had been a huge concession on her part.

It wasn't just Nori's actions, though, that had given him a place amongst the fey. Thanks to his connection to the Lost Well and his passing of a series of impossible trials, Aleks had won favor with the Autumn Court, or at least with its commoners.

Having sent diplomatic teams to deliver word to the other courts that a new connection had been forged to the well, he'd soon gather the support of the remaining three courts, no matter how unlikely it was. He'd have to sort out the true friends from the sycophants. If he could do it quickly, all the better. His neck was on the line – literally.

Changelings were not allowed inside Niffleheim. If spotted, they were to be killed on sight. Through luck, prayer, and carefully worded promises, Aleks still lived. If nothing else, it was in their laws to support a proven claim for the Lost Well.

Some would do so to curry favor, others to save face. He wasn't naïve enough to believe all would happily submit to him, but he hoped to have the commoners on his side; and through their numbers, force the nobles' hands, even though they weren't so pleased with this turn of events, his own father being one of them.

Unthinkingly, Aleks glanced backward, searching for the dwarves. He knew the moment he'd been spotted. It had only taken a split-second, such a small mistake, but it had been enough. One of the warriors pointed in his direction and shouted. He turned around, but it was too late. They had seen their torches reflected in his eyes.

"We need to split," Aleks hissed, just as his spotter cried out, "They're getting away!"

It had sounded like Frigga.

He could hardly believe all this was over one simple arrow meant for a different target.

That dwarf could hold a grudge.

Chapter Two: A Wish Granted

As they ran, Aleks berated himself for his lack of caution, cursing himself all kinds of fool. Henrik had warned them, and he, too wrapped up in his own thoughts, had gone and done the very thing he wasn't supposed to do. Clearly, Christoffer didn't have a lock on poor decisions today or was it tomorrow by now?

He needed sleep and the chance to get back on an even keel. The dwarves relentlessly pursued them across the plains. Their rhythmic marching created a hypnotic lull. Aleks felt his eyes drift down, and despite his efforts couldn't stop their fall. He forced himself to open them, staring sightlessly into the dim surroundings around him.

He struggled to keep them open; he even imagined toothpicks prying his eyelids apart, his mind processing the scenery as if in slow motion. As they scurried like mice from a prowling cat, he again recognized where they were. But some force weighed on his tongue, and he was too foggy to tell Henrik he had missed the turn and was going the wrong way. Aleks reached out for someone, seeing the shadow of them ahead, but empty air met his grasping hand. Losing his balance, he pitched forward and collapsed on the ground, seeing red light behind his eyelids.

As soon as he landed, Aleks forced back a curse. His mind whirled as a fresh round of adrenaline shot through him. He gasped for breath and found his tongue working again. He licked his parched lips, hoping to form a word. Why was he so tired?

"Wrong way," he croaked, clearing his throat. "You're going the wrong way."

They had gone too far. Nobody heard him. He couldn't risk pitching his voice louder and drawing the dwarves' attention. He swallowed and listened, trying to see how far they had gone. Strange, he couldn't hear his friends or the dwarves.

He shifted, and the movement caused a dreaded metallic *clink, clink, clink*. His eyes shot open, watering and drying out by equal measures, forcing him to blink rapidly. He rubbed them with the back of his hand. Above, a faint circle glowed. He shook his head, trying to dislodge the image, but the faint circle remained. His stomach twisted in knots.

"We really have to stop meeting like this," Aleks told the well at large. "I can't keep waking up here."

The Lost Well was, as usual, a silent companion in the predawn gloom. Yawning, Aleks forced himself to his feet, wobbling on unsteady legs. He was still ridiculously tired, but somehow felt refreshed. He stared at the gold and silver stacks of coins and objects glittering around his feet. He didn't see his raven anywhere. Usually she was here somewhere, pestering him to wake up.

"Airi?" he called, turning around in a circle looking for her, expecting to find her asleep with her head tucked under a wing.

Her absence gnawed at him ominously. Aleks frowned. He didn't like that they were separated. It was as though the world had gone off-kilter. Something might have gone wrong. Had Airi reached his sister in time to rescue his friends? He could only hope, as he couldn't help from here. He'd first have to figure out how to make his way back to them.

Something glowed at the top of a small mound of objects and coins. That was new. Aleks moved toward it, but stopped to glance upwards, checking on the encroaching sun. He couldn't risk getting trapped. Still seeing moonlight, he scrambled up the shifting pile of fairy loot.

He discovered the glowing object to be a silvery open-faced helmet. Aleks snatched it up with a certain amount of shock. From the interior shone a distorted, but recognizable face with thick, dark eyebrows and a freshly broken nose. Blood covered the entire bottom half of Falkor's face, as if he were a particularly messy vampire and not the mountain-troll he most certainly was.

Falkor was one of the firstborn trolls Aleks and his friends had rescued from the dungeons of Trolgar, and he, in turn, had saved them from the Wild Hunt. He came from the Bow-Legged Nose Basher House, which probably explained his newly broken nose. Aleks bet they smashed each other in the face instead of hugging to show affection. That seemed like a normal troll thing to do.

"Is this thing on?" the troll asked, a big finger coming up to tap on his distorted nose. "Hello? Anyone there?"

Aleks grinned, angling the mirror so the large teen could see him. "Falkor, you found the mirror!"

The finger disappeared, and Falkor leaned in closer. "Oh hey, Aleks. Yes, we found the mirror."

The mirror in question was a magical one that showed the user someone they sought out. It had been found by Christoffer in a dwarvish junk shop called the Hidden Gem, run by the kindhearted, if slightly batty, Granny. A few days ago it had been stolen by Jorkden, acting king of Trolgar and an all around jerk, when he had captured Aleks and his friends outside the trolls' city.

"What's going on?" asked Aleks, checking the skyline again for hints of dawn.

"We're going to attempt a jail-break," said Falkor.

Kafirr, the true troll king, waited, trapped in the dungeons, for a chance to fight for his crown. He'd been down there for over a year as Jorkden tried to diminish his foe's strength. The Wild Hunt leader had every right to fear such a fight, because Kafirr was massive (trolls prized rulers by their size), and as a member from the Iron-Bellied Stone Eaters House had a magical connection to the cave in which the troll capital resided.

The iron, which he ate from within the cave, gave him power over the formation of the cave. Except for that very same iron, Kafirr could create anything, move anything, and destroy anything inside the cave using the earth and rocks. The iron also had the effect of turning his teeth and nails black from carving it out and chewing it. It made for a very intimidating look which villains everywhere would envy, although in this tale he wasn't currently a villain at all (apparently he'd been one, or at the very least self-serving in the far distant past before Aleks' had been born, but that was neither here nor there.)

As much as Jorkden would wish it, he couldn't just have Kafirr killed. He had to fight Kafirr one-on-one in a death match in order to claim for real what he falsely claimed now. With the deck stacked against him, was it any wonder Jorkden played dirty? He'd been tossing the firstborn children of the noble houses into the dungeon when their families disobeyed him. He'd done the same to Kafirr, sticking him in an iron-lined cell, eliminating direct contact with the cave, so he couldn't wield it to escape. If solitary imprisonment wasn't enough, Jorkden starved Kafirr for over a year in an attempt to weaken him before the fight.

Aleks had accidentally led everyone to Kafirr in the dungeons, and Zaria had rustled up some grub for the troll king to supplement his iron diet. Then, with a little direction from Kafirr, they had found the firstborn, the children of the troll king's allies, and freed them.

When the fight came, as it was bound to come, Jorkden would be in for a big surprise as Kafirr would not be the weakling that he expected, but a force to reckon with. The firstborn safe, Kafirr would be able to unleash his full abilities. So, too, would his allies, who led the resistance against Jorkden's tyranny, as they also would be out in full strength, free from oppression and fear for their heirs' lives. The reign of Jorkden would be blessedly brief and quick to topple.

A new face appeared in the mirror. A rainbow-haired girl with long ears and a bone-white eyebrow piercing grinned back at him. The teenage troll had paired with Aleks during the escape from Trolgar and Jorkden's planned feast, featuring the flesh and bones of Aleks and his friends as the main course. Together, he and Zorka had outwitted more than one sharp-toothed beast while escaping the Wild Hunt, and they had formed a friendship in the process. He waved to her.

"We could really use your help," she said, and without skipping a beat, added, "You look funny, Aleks. Why is that?"

He laughed. "It's because I'm looking at you from inside a helmet."

She made a face. "Then find something better. You're looking pinched. It's like seeing a mouse or something. Very off-putting. At least be a cat."

"Give me a second," he told her.

He glanced around the Lost Well. There were mounds of coins everywhere. Poking through the heaps of gold and silver were jewels, cups, plates, candlesticks, and other objects, which the fey in yesteryears had tossed into the well as a bribe for granting wishes. He laid the helmet aside, went over to one of the plates sticking out, and gave it a sharp tug, nearly falling backwards on his rear when the thing didn't budge.

Aleks peered closer and saw that his plate was not a dish, but another piece of armor. He dug the breastplate out from under the coins and tangled jewelry that weighed it down. The first thing he noticed was that the back of it was made of leather. There were even straps to tighten it to fit its wearer. Not a speck of rust discolored its surface. It was truly in excellent condition for being periodically submerged in water for hours at a time. The bottom part of the front, below the chest area, imitated dragon scales.

"How's this?" he asked, looking down onto its polished surface.

Zorka considered him and nodded. "You're still lumpy in places, but you're no longer pinched."

"You look better, too," he said, warmly. "Tell me more about this jail-break. How can we help?"

Her grin turned feral. "Jorkden is rip-roaring mad that we firstborn are still at large. He's been tossing innocents into the dungeons in an attempt to locate us. We're ready to bring the fight to him."

"We're splitting up into a multipronged attack," Falkor began.

Zorka pushed him aside. "I'm on this lug's team. We're in charge of the distraction. It's going to be brilliant."

Falkor stuck his head back in the frame. "I'm hoping you will help us by confusing the wolves and wolverines. As you know, under Jorkden's command, the Wild Hunt is paused, but never stopped. If the animals get hold of your scent, they'll add to the confusion by chasing the wrong targets."

"If we're the bait what will you be doing?"

"Setting off bombs," Falkor said conspiratorially.

Aleks' eyebrows winged up toward his hairline in surprise. "You're not worried about the destruction? You could cause a cave-in and crush everyone beneath the earth."

"Nah," the burly teen said. "Kafirr will fix anything we do when he's back in power. It'll only be a mild inconvenience."

"As fun as it would be to be bait," said Aleks, scratching his neck, "I'm afraid we're in a pickle over here. King Flein sent a contingent of soldiers to shut down further fey aggression."

Zorka's eyes lit up. "The Ravagers by any chance?" she asked, almost pressing her nose to the mirror in her enthusiasm.

"Are they an all-female troop?" asked Aleks, leaning back to try to bring her face into perspective. At her nod, he added, "Then, yes."

She clasped her hands in front of her, practically swooning. "Oh, what I'd give to fight them in a real battle. Those ladies are deadly adversaries on the battle field. They're said to use their bare hands to rip out the innards of their enemies."

He grimaced. "We would like our innards to remain where they are, thank you very much."

She sighed dramatically. "You have all the luck, getting to face off against legends. We only have dumb old Jorkden, some hags, and some banshees."

"Only that, huh? Any chance of you wanting to come here?"

"Oh, I wish I could," she said. "As fun as Falkor's group is, I'd rather be there. A troll hasn't been to Niffleheim in years and years and years."

Aleks ran a hand through his hair, untangling a lock and dislodging a coin. He flicked it away. "I wish you were here, too. We could use the help. I'm not sure we'll get this sorted out before you need –"

A flame of red magic erupted in a column before him. Yelling in alarm, Aleks dropped the breastplate and scrambled away, shielding his face from the blaze. When the heat dissipated, he cautiously lowered his arm and looked at the spot where he had just been crouching. Before him stood a very surprised Zorka with her claws out.

"What are you doing here?" he asked, just as she said, "How did I get here?"

Aleks shook his head dumbly. "I have no idea."

"Is this the Lost Well?" she asked, twirling a lock of cotton-candy pink hair. She spun in a circle. "I've heard stories about this place."

Aleks scratched his neck. "Yes, um…"

He was interrupted by a frantic Falkor shouting, "Zorka just disappeared! In a column of flame! What fresh crazy is this? As if I don't have enough to deal with right now."

Aleks lunged to the breastplate and brought it level to his gaze. "Zorka's here."

Checked, Falkor ceased shouting for a minute. Then he roared, "Changeling, this is not the help I asked for! Send her back!"

Feeling like a chastened schoolboy, Aleks resisted the urge to duck. "It's not like I had anything to do with it," he said hotly. "She's the one that showed up out of the blue... er... red."

Zorka cleared her throat. "Actually, you did wish me here. Your bond with the well lets you do some extraordinary things. Just please don't force me to travel by flame again." She touched her flushed cheeks. "If you do, I just might be turned into Gisken's sister with red marks all up and down my body. I would not make a good Red-Throated member. I much prefer pink to blood-red."

"Wishing? I didn't – I didn't mean – wait – how do you know the well bonded to me?" asked Aleks.

She indicated the room at large and then pointed to herself. "I'm here, aren't I? Proof in point."

"Zorka is essential to tonight's plan," Falkor growled. "I need my right-hand woman."

She tittered. "Don't let Knottie hear you, or your nose will be permanently broken."

Falkor rubbed the bruised bridge abashedly. "My girl certainly has a temper."

Zorka rolled her eyes. Looking at Aleks, she said conspiratorially, "She didn't like him picking me over her to go with him on tonight's mission."

"I love her, but the girl's a distraction. I wouldn't be able to focus with her nearby."

Zorka jerked her chin toward the breastplate. "Can you believe this troll? It's his own fault he can't keep his hands to himself when he's around her."

"It's her fault when she doesn't keep hers to herself," said Falkor, adding petulantly, "She starts it."

"You don't have to try and finish it," she huffed.

"I know! Why do you think I picked you to come with me tonight?" Falkor groused.

Aleks looked skyward again and saw that the edges of the well's opening were shimmering in warning. He nudged Zorka. "Should I try sending you home? We don't have much time."

"Before what?" She followed his gaze. "Oh, it's going to close. Can you send me home later? I want to fight the Ravagers and rub Kanutte's face in it."

"Not later. Not later. Abort!" shouted Falkor, impotently.

Aleks frowned. "I'm not even sure I can send you home *now*. Wishing you here might have been a fluke."

Zorka peered over Aleks' shoulder. "Hear that, Falkor? A fluke! Toodle-loo," she singsonged to her friend.

His eyes widened. "What? No! Aleks!"

But the decision was made and there was no backing down now. Aleks pointed her to the low tunnel connecting the bottom of the well to the fey's manufactured void. She nodded, but went in the opposite direction. He stared agape as she bent to fetch the helmet.

"Leave it," Aleks told her. "We have to hurry!"

She ignored him, taking the helmet with her. He moved to drop the breastplate, but she forced him to bring it with him through the tunnel. Aleks didn't argue, knowing he could give them back from the other side. He scrambled out, and turned to see about helping Zorka through. She was wider than the tunnel, and taller, but he thought if Henrik's and Hector's antlered cloaks could wedge through, perhaps the teenage troll could, too.

As she crawled, the tunnel widened like an expanding bubble, shocking him, although upon reflection it didn't seem strange. In moments, she was standing up, flicking her rainbow hair aside. Aleks watched the tunnel ripple and sway, visibly shrinking. Jolted from his trance, he got to the task at hand, shaking coins from his clothes. As they dropped he kicked them into the pile spilling out from the well's tunnel.

"You should do the same," he said, as the opening wavered and rippled in agitation and pending closure. "Hurry, or the well will claim you, trapping you to it."

He snatched the helmet from her and attempted to throw it and the breastplate back. Zorka checked him hard, sending him sprawling and the pieces of armor flying. He struggled to his feet and stared in mute horror as the well's entrance vanished, leaving him with two unwanted pieces of fairy armor.

"Why did you do that?" he asked her, furious. "I've been so careful not to take anything from the well that wasn't mine."

She picked up the breastplate, dusting it off. "Because, once you're bonded to the well, everything in it belongs to you. If we're taking on a bunch of overzealous female dwarf warriors, you're going to need protection, little fox."

Aleks crossed his arms, refusing to touch the armor. "You know an awful lot about the well," he accused.

She grinned, unaffected by his surliness. "We learn this in grade school, just in case the protections on the well break, and its wild magic gets back into the fey's hands. Know your enemy as they say."

Nonplussed, Aleks closed his mouth with a snap. "Sure, okay. The Lost Well is troll school curriculum. That makes perfect sense, but how do you know that it's bonded to me? Don't you dare say it's because I summoned you."

She took an exaggerated sniff over his hair. "Its magic clings to you like an extra layer of skin. You're no longer a disowned thing. How could I not sense it? It smells like gold."

"Gold doesn't have a scent," he groused, accepting the breastplate reluctantly. "Also, I take offense. I am not disowned. I have a wonderful human family, loyal friends, and a magnificent white raven."

"The fey disowned you is all I meant," she said, bending to pick up the helmet. She spat on its crown and rubbed it with the edge of her sleeve. "That is no longer true, as their magic has claimed you."

"And the gold smell?" he pressed.

"Fine, not gold," Zorka said, rolling her eyes. "Its magic on you smells noble then. One might even say, kingly. What do you think?"

"I think the Lost Well is playing a practical joke on me. I never wanted this, you know."

Zorka stared down at him. "You've got it now. Might as well make use of it. Put this on."

Uncaringly, Aleks shoved his head into the opening on the armor and tugged it down. He took the proffered helmet and placed it on his head. "I feel ridiculous," he told her.

Her smile was full of teeth. "You look it, too, like a child playing dress-up. You have to tighten the straps on your armor."

When he did, the armor shrunk in size, fitting snugly. While the leather on the back gave him some mobility, the metallic breastplate molded to him like a hardened shell. He twisted around, testing its range and limits. "Not bad. Might be better for a swordsman. As an archer, I need a little more range."

"Doesn't the leather give it to you?" Zorka asked. "You look respectable in it now that it's sized appropriately."

Aleks pulled a face, twisting and turning, trying to bend the leather. "It's not the same. I like being able to move when I must."

"Quit complaining. It'll keep you alive," she said, adding, "You're puny. You need all the help you can get. Your skin isn't like a mountain-troll's. You bleed quite easily."

He chose not to comment on that, for it was true that a mountain-troll's skin was tougher than a lot of substances – granite, marble, limestone – basically anything stone-like. Bullets rarely did more than bother them, merely grazing as they passed by. Giants were probably the only other beings that could go head-to-head or fist-to-fist against them in a fight, as they were actually made of stone.

"Now what?" he asked, disliking wearing the helmet as it slid down his face. He pushed it back to see better.

Her eyes lit up. She pulled a couple of wrapped packages from her pockets. "What do you say we set loose some bombs in Niffleheim?"

"Why are all the girls I know so bloodthirsty?" he muttered under his breath. "You know Kafirr isn't here to fix anything that goes wrong, right?"

She heard, and guffawed heartily, her long ears twitching in amusement. "Come on, Changeling, let's wreak havoc on those Ravagers."

"Are the bombs deadly?" he asked, gingerly taking a package between his fingers. "How much destruction do they cause? I'm trying to stop a war with the dwarves, not start one in earnest."

Zorka tied her ears behind her head. "They're deadly…" she tapped her nose, "but only to your olfactory senses."

Aleks blinked. "These are stink bombs? But Falkor said Kafirr would have to fix the destruction later."

Her eyes lit up with understanding. "We have those bombs, too. Falkor's real choosy about them. Only he and Kanutte are allowed to work with those. I was put in charge of these babies," she said, raising the packages for emphasis.

"To throw the Wild Hunt off their targets?" he guessed.

She nodded enthusiastically. "Modolf even has some dry ice grenades to detonate with Regnor. A nice smoke-out will blind those banshees and hags, real good, don't you think? My friends will never miss these stinkers and we can put them to good use."

A mischievous smile quirked upwards on his face as he pictured Brunhild's expression after inhaling the stink bomb at point-blank range. He said, "Let's go prank some dwarves."

"That's the spirit, little fox," Zorka said, smiling wolfishly. "Watch out. We'll make a troll out of you yet. You'll see."

Chapter Three: Eau de Troll is All the Rage

By the time Aleks and Zorka caught up to the dwarves, sunlight filtered through the icy scalloped ceiling, suffusing the plains in pale gray light. It dappled across the walls and floors, with undulating patterns that reminded Aleks of being underwater.

The dwarves were excited and whipped into a frenzy having cornered their targets. Aleks cursed, knowing their quarry to be his friends. Edging closer, he spied Henrik out front, knocking spears out of the air with his broad sword. Zaria zapped away more than her fair share as well, but the assault was unceasing, and even with the two of them working in tandem, spears slipped by their defenses. Geirr yelped, dodging a spear headed straight for him, managing only to get grazed as it passed his shoulder, ripping the fabric.

"Zaria, watch it! I almost got skewered," Geirr complained, poking his finger in the hole.

Christoffer dodged another spear, and collapsed, folding over with hands on knees. Winded, he joked, "Yeah, Zaria. We didn't decline the troll's dinner invitation only to be shish-kabobbed by the dwarves. Wipe the floor with them already."

"You two try stopping dozens of spears all at once. I'd bet you'd miss some, too," she groused. "Everyone's a critic."

"Come on Zar-Zar, stop playing nice," Filip urged.

"I can only do so much at once," she said, turning to look at them.

"Watch out, Princess!" Henrik warned, pushing her out of the way as a spear sailed through the space where she'd been standing.

Filip gulped, pushing her to face the front. "Okay. Okay. Eyes on the dwarves. Just *please* be safe."

Aleks itched to join them, but knew that would only put more pressure on Zaria. There had to be a way to help. He frowned, surveying the scene. It really was odd that no matter how many spears the dwarves launched, they seemed to have an endless supply. Magic must be delivering that effect. If he could locate it, maybe he could stop it. He canvassed the troop for something out of the ordinary.

Zorka pointed one long finger toward the middle of the brigade. *Bingo!* In the center, two dwarves pulled spears from a nearly empty sack before handing them to runners, who in turn passed them to throwers — stocky dwarf women with powerful broad shoulders and arms thick as tree branches. New spears kept reappearing in the sack's opening every time a set was pulled free. The sack emptied only to be instantly refilled. This was the source of their weapons.

"We need to get that sack," said Zorka.

"No lie," Aleks agreed. "Do you have a plan?"

She turned to him, whispering, "I say we lob a stink bomb right into the heart of their group and see if it scatters them."

"We'll have to race so we can steal the sack, or they might return once they realize it is just smoke."

"You haven't smelled Regnor's patented stink bombs," she said, light glinting off her brow piercing like a wink. "Nobody can breathe it in without fainting. Kanutte's tried. Funniest thing you've ever seen in your life – seeing her keel over, feet up."

"I'd pay to see that," he said. "Okay. We'll hold our breath when we go. We can't risk the dwarves regrouping. How many should we launch?"

"One will probably do it," Zorka said, unwrapping one of her precious packages.

As the canvas wrap was peeled back, Aleks' eyes instantly watered. It was worse than a thousand onions being chopped at once; worse than a thousand mildewed towels, soaked in sweat; worse than a thousand unwashed, sockless feet just out of their shoes, and it hadn't even been lit. He coughed, hiding his nose in his sleeve.

"Those *are* deadly," he squeaked, trying not to breathe in more of it.

She patted her pockets looking for something, sniffing slightly as her nose began to run. "I hear he uses his own awful stench from his workouts. Musk and perspiration, the very best ingredients for eau de troll. It's going to be glorious. Aha!"

Zorka presented a match the size of a small dowel. She struck it against the wall and lit the fuse on the stink bomb. "Oh Ravagers!" she singsonged, calling their attention. "Bombs away!"

Brunhild and a few others turned to see them as Zorka lobbed the stink bomb with the force and speed of a shotput thrower. Had she been a dwarf they would've been proud, but as it was, they were annoyed at her presence.

Even though her accuracy was a little off she managed to hit one of the runners, mid-pass. The dwarf dropped the armful of spears she was juggling, just as the bomb went off with a loud *BANG!*

Thick, sulfurous, yellow smoke billowed out like a cloud, diminishing sight better than a raging sandstorm. Aleks and Zorka ran into the midst. He bounced off choking dwarves, as they wailed and moaned, running away from the smoke, some fainting on the spot just as Zorka predicted. Determined to get to the enchanted sack, Aleks pushed past them, headfirst into the stench. It was as if his eyes had hidden olfactory receptors. They leaked faster, the smoky air practically pulling tears out with its sheer pungency. His nose burned like the hairs were being singed off.

Zorka and Aleks shoved and dodged dwarves respectively, making their way into the heart of the troop. Over the chaos and din, Brunhild could be heard issuing commands. They came out in staccato, all sharp and pointed, flung with rancor. Dwarves struggled to carry them, but Zorka knocked everyone over as if they were bowling pins giving way under the force of a cannonball. They ricocheted everywhere, sending helmets and braids flying in opposite directions.

"Where did that damn troll come from?" snarled Brunhild. Her voice sounded clogged from breathing in the noxious fumes. "Take her down. NOW!"

Over it all, Aleks could hear his friends stumbling around, equally affected by the assault. He looked for them, trying to pierce the smoke with his gaze. It was like keeping his eyes open in saltwater, itchy and uncomfortable.

"Over here," Aleks croaked, trying to direct them with the last of his fresh air.

He had no idea whether they heard him because at the same time, Henrik sneezed like a great big goose.

Christoffer kept saying, "My eyes, my eyes, it burns!"

"Cover your nose," Geirr said, coughing.

"Covered," wheezed Filip. "Zar-Zar, a breeze, please?"

Air began flowing. Aleks could feel it against his legs. He had to hurry. He had not yet found the sack. Wiping away his tears, he peered around blearily. His lungs burned with the need to breathe. He went to pull his shirt up over his face only to hit the metal front of his new armor.

Cursing his luck, he took a hesitant breath and felt like a landed fish gasping at air. The very air was moist and thick, as if Regnor's sweat had fogged the room. Panic seized him. He couldn't breathe. The air by his ankles shifted again and he dove for it, inhaling the clean air in great gulps.

"A little help," Zorka grunted. "Ouch. Stop that!"

Ten dwarves had latched onto her, clinging to various body parts. Two clung to her right leg. One sat on her left foot, holding her ankle. Five hung from her arms like weights. One gripped her neck in a chokehold, causing Zorka's eyes to bulge. The last one sat on her head, tugging on her tied-ears. She wobbled drunkenly, tilting in the direction the dwarf pulled her ears.

Just then Aleks spied the sack. Brunhild spotted him as he made a move for it. They eyed each other up and then as one, both lunged at the same time, clunking heads. Grateful for the helmet, Aleks shook his head, clearing out the ringing in his ears. He grabbed the sack, meeting resistance as the lieutenant tugged on it, too. They stared at each other over the cloth.

Unamused, Brunhild yanked hard. "Let go," she snarled at him.

"You let go," he countered, pulling harder.

With a swift tug, he sent them sprawling backwards on the dirt. Folding up the sack, Aleks stood. By now the smoke had cleared even more. Through the haze, he could make out shapes and other colors besides yellow. Ravagers were beginning to collect their wits, their coughing and choking easing, as did his own. Henrik's antlered cloak loomed high over the dwarves' heads. He still had his elbow over his face, blocking the smell.

"Henrik!" Aleks shouted. "Grab the others!"

"Aleks-AH? CHOO!" he called, sneezing halfway through. "Aleks, is that you?"

He tucked the empty sack down the neck of his armor, feeling like a stuffed shirt, literally. "Zorka needs help! They're all over her!"

"Zorka?" Henrik asked, confused. "How did she get here?"

"Not important right now!" shouted Aleks, barreling toward Zorka and the dwarves.

The dwarf on her head, noticing him, tugged on her ears. Zorka flailed, snarling a bone-chilling, blood-curdling sound of rage. Against her will she followed the command like a horse steered by its rider. Aleks tried to stop, but his momentum carried him and he slammed straight into the backs of her knees.

With a shout, Zorka wobbled dangerously. He grabbed hold of her knotted belt, but the rainbow-haired troll kept tipping precariously forward. The dwarves recognizing danger, leapt off her like sailors escaping a sinking vessel. The belt snapped and she plummeted headfirst, barely able to bring her hands up to shield her face from the ground.

"Zorka!" he shouted, pulling the tetchy Ravager from her head. "Are you all right?"

"Do you have the sack?" she asked, nodding absently at his yes, and spitting out a tooth. "Drat, now I'll look lopsided. You're going to pay for that, you wretched dwarf!"

"We'll worry about the Ravagers later. Can you stand? I can't lift you," said Aleks, by her elbow.

Zorka grunted, shifting onto her knees and standing with a push. "Where are the rest of you?"

Aleks pointed to Henrik shepherding his friends through the disgruntled mob of Ravagers. "We don't have much time before Brunhild gets her troop in order."

She lumbered toward the others, untying her ears and rubbing her scalp. Threads of rainbow hair fell to the floor as she combed. She didn't seem to notice. Aleks waved at his friends to get their attention. Zaria waved back, relief spreading across her face.

Christoffer ran over, plugging his nose as he came closer. "Vas vat vou?" he croaked.

"It was all Regnor," said Zorka, waggling her eyebrows. "Why do you think we always say he stinks?"

"Don't tell me you have more of those stink bombs," said Christoffer, letting go of his nose, though keeping his breath shallow. "They should be classed as chemical weapons."

Aleks' laugh was watery. He cleared his throat, trying to remove phlegm. "It did the trick. We have to get out of the plains and back to court."

"That's what we were doing until you disappeared, man," said Geirr, reproachfully. "Dude, what's up with your fancy get-up?"

"Stole the words right out of my mouth," said Christoffer, with a cheeky knock against his helmet "What happened, Aleks? One minute you were there, and the next you disappeared in a wall of flame. What happened?"

"The well pulled me back," said Aleks. "I guess I have a curfew or something."

"Like Cinderella," said Zaria, her eyes lighting up.

"Who?" scoffed Zorka. "Who is Cindy Rella? Sounds like a Daisy Pusher to me."

Zaria shook her head. "Cinderella, she's a –" A spear lodged at her feet, halting her explanation of the fairy-tale character. She snapped her mouth closed in anger. With two hands, she grabbed the spear, withdrew it from the ground, and hurled it back with all her might, yelling, "WE ARE NOT YOUR ENEMIES!"

"Damn, Zar-Zar," said Filip, taking her hand and pulling her along. He turned to watch over his shoulder as the spear landed with remarkable accuracy between Brunhild's booted feet. "Remind me never to get on your bad side."

"You can say that again," said Christoffer, jogging beside them.

As she ran, Zaria tucked flyaways back into the crown of hair braided around her face. Her purple eyes flashed with steel. "Just because I'm a princess doesn't mean I'm not scary."

"Princess," called Brunhild, her words carrying clearly across the cavern. Zaria looked back at the lieutenant, wariness etched across every line of her face. The dwarf, seeing she had Zaria's attention, warned, "One more attack from you, and the dwarves won't be beholden to the Dragomir Treaty. We will not be gentle with backstabbing traitorous witches."

"Is that supposed to be an insult?" Zaria asked. "Because I've met the witch of the woods. I'll take the comparison as a compliment."

Sneering, Brunhild grasped the flank of the spear and with her boot snapped it in two. Zaria's nostrils flared, and her magic glowed around her like a halo. She stopped, intending to turn and march straight back into the fray, when Aleks, grabbing her shirt collar, jerked her to a halt.

"We can stand off later. Stow the magic," he ordered.

She blew out a frustrated breath. "Why doesn't that woman — that *lieutenant* — see that I am not her enemy? That we're not fighting her Ravagers, but protecting ourselves from them?"

"Fritjof," Henrik said, knowing that this explained everything. And it did.

"Damn dragons," muttered Filip.

"Follow me," said Aleks, herding his friends along. "We're close. We just have to backtrack a bit."

"Are you sure?" asked Geirr. "Like, really sure? We can't be wrong. We won't escape again."

Consternation kept Aleks from replying. He'd known it was only a matter of time before his friends caught on and demanded a new navigator. Feeling impotent, he clenched his fists and looked away. What could he say? Geirr was right, he wasn't *sure,* but he was sure.

"Geirr," said Zaria, reaching out with supplicating hands to them both. "Not now, okay? We follow Aleks as usual."

Looking at Aleks' firm jaw and tight mouth, Geirr relaxed and nodded. He said, "At least in the daylight we'll know if we're heading the wrong way."

"Thanks for the vote of confidence," Aleks ground out, feeling hurt despite knowing his friend had a right to question him. He hadn't been very good at navigating lately, but that wasn't a reason to doubt him now.

"You two can hash this out later," said Zaria. "Let's get out of here."

"Who would have guessed that the Autumn Court would be a safe haven for us?" Henrik mused, the first to follow Aleks as he led them back through the plains.

"Stranger things have happened," said Zaria.

At the sounds of Brunhild's troop beating their breastplates, Aleks kicked into a jog. With their war cries in his ears, the little group ran. Zorka generously took the rearward position to protect them from any spears that might come their way. Being thick-skinned certainly had its advantages in a retreat.

The ground vibrated as the Ravagers stomped in pursuit. The dwarves didn't have to run to catch up. With so few features in the plains, there was no hiding from them. Every move he and his friends made could be seen... and followed.

The most skilled of their throwers tossed their spears. Whistling through the air, they embedded with a twang into the bedrock and walls. More grateful than ever to have Zorka at his back, Aleks sprinted forward, trying to gain distance. Christoffer groaned beside him for the wicked pace he set.

Aiming for one of the high spots with a bright hazy outline, Aleks guided his friends the last dozen feet. Behind this wall in the narrow corridor was a low tunnel, which led to the Autumn Court. They were close to help now; Aleks could feel it.

The dwarves, sensing their quarry might be slipping through their fingers, broke into a run. The racket from their armor echoed off the cavern's walls in a dizzying, disorienting din. Filip covered his ears, running with his elbows sticking out like a crazed chicken. It would've been funny if it hadn't chilled Aleks to his marrow to hear it.

Knowing his friends were right behind, Aleks pushed through the burning in his calves. In a shift of light, he transformed into his fox form, and blitzed around the corner and down the tunnel. The warm light from the court ahead spilled through the tunnel, brighter and clearer than the silvery liquid light from the cave at his back.

He knew if he could get to the other side, he'd find Airi waiting with help. He knew in his gut she'd gotten him the help he'd asked for, but he had a new message for her now. All of fey needed to be warned and prepare for an invasion. Everyone who couldn't fight had to get to safety. Surely with the skulk of foxes and fey on the other side of this tunnel, Brunhild would turn aside and retreat. Her small brigade had no hope of victory.

Aleks shifted again as he reached the Autumn Court. Standing and scanning the fields for his raven, Aleks was shocked to find that no Airi waited for him. Equally missing, Nori. Not a soul stirred in the morning light. The dirty haze, which hung over the nearby city like a malaise, mocked him, saying he should've known better than to trust the fey.

"Aleks are you out there?" asked Zaria, poking her head out of the tunnel. Seeing him, she ducked back, shouting, "He's here! How are we going to get Zorka through?" she asked, accepting his hand to stand up.

"We have a bigger problem," he spat out. "Nobody's here. Did Airi not give my sister the message?"

She looked around him, searching the broken cityscape. When she met his eyes, concern etched her purple gaze. "We won't make it to the Rød Skyttergraven if the dwarves come through the tunnel after us. I will have to use my magic again."

"Is that the plan?" asked Filip, as he crawled out next.

"I hope not," she said, turning from Aleks to help him stand, pressing a light kiss to his cheek.

He blushed beet red, casting a shy glance at her beneath blond eyelashes. "Hey Zar-Zar," he said, brushing off a smudge of dirt from her cheek with his thumb.

"You two have got it so bad," said Christoffer, catching them in the act. "I can't decide if it's cute or nauseating."

"Cute," Zaria decreed, giving Filip another peck, this time her kiss landing on his lips.

"Nauseating," Geirr teased, following Christoffer out.

Filip cleared his throat, wrapping an arm around Zaria's waist, and said, "Stuff it, mate."

"Zorka's still on the other side," Zaria reminded the group.

Aleks frowned, turning his attention to the problem at hand. "Can you shrink her?"

Zaria cast him a wry glance, her eyes twinkling as she said, "Christoffer made that suggestion, and she flat out told me that her right hook is worse than Kanutte's. So, no, I can't shrink her."

Henrik ducked through the tunnel. "Trolls prize themselves by their size. You take away that and it's like taking away who they are."

"She'd give it right back," Christoffer complained.

"Zaria's bruise from Kanutte is just now fading, so no way," said Filip, giving her waist a squeeze. "There's got to be another way to get her through the tunnel.

"Perhaps we can put her on something so she can lay flat, maybe we can pull her out?" offered Geirr. "Like a creeper or a blanket or something?"

"It's worth a shot," said Zaria. "Let's try the one with wheels, first."

Between one blink and the next a large flat creeper appeared, with a long rope attached. It was broad enough to fit nearly the entire width of the tunnel, and long enough to fit a teenage troll on her stomach, if she kept her feet up and away from the ground.

Aleks bit his tongue to keep from admonishing Zaria for using her magic without her fake-out hand signals.

With Fritjof this close at hand, she shouldn't be so careless. With all of fey watching him and his friends, it was potentially disastrous.

Instead, he joined Christoffer and Geirr as they took one side of the creeper, while Filip and Henrik took the other. Together, they wrangled it into place, and pushed it through toward Zorka's ankles. She yelped in surprise, leaping forward when it tapped against her. Spinning around, she crouched down and peered through the tunnel.

Aleks waved. "Get on that, and we'll pull you."

"I'm too tall," she said. "Even sitting." With a grunt, she batted away a spear. "Plus, the Ravagers are here."

"Good thing your skin's nearly impenetrable," said Christoffer. At Aleks' stern look, he shrugged. "What? It's true."

"Get on your stomach," Aleks instructed. "Kick them if they try to come through behind you."

Reluctantly, Zorka followed instructions and positioned herself on the creeper. She cursed a string of words and phrases nearly as colorful as her hair, as more spears were tossed at her. Kicking and writhing, she lashed out at the dwarves circling the tunnel's entrance. Her thrashing nearly tipped the creeper over on its side. If it had, she'd have been wedged in place like a bottle stopper.

"Stop flailing," Filip told her. "If you keep it up, we won't be able to pull you."

"Why don't you try being a pincushion?" she snarled. "See how still you are, when you get pricked. I can't believe I said I wanted to be here more than in Trolgar. Wretched she-beasts. I. Hate. Dwarves."

Aleks would've stopped their bickering, but Christoffer began taunting her, telling her that she made for a bad troll letting such small creatures ruin her fearsome reputation. As Zorka stopped flailing he kept going, ignoring her thunderous glare. Her face clouded, as storm clouds gathered behind her eyes.

Aleks shook his head. His smart-mouth friend would have to watch himself or he'd get smacked when she got free. But his teasing did the trick, distracting her from the attacks at her feet. Zorka took his words for a challenge and held herself stiller than a predator seconds before springing an attack.

With one last grunt of effort, the five of them hauled her out of the tunnel. She slid forward, squealing as it raced downhill like a sled across snow. Zaria ran after her, wringing her hands, clearly not sure if she should magic the creeper away or let it run its course.

Filip, Christoffer, and Geirr chased after them, racing down, arms akimbo as if to stop the troll in her tracks. Zorka toppled over with a great big crash, sending the creeper flying into the distance. Aleks watched it sail through the air, shielding his eyes to track its course.

"We need to get away from here," shouted Henrik, pushing Aleks out of the way. "Brunhild's warriors are in the tunnel."

The sounds of armor clanging, brought him to his senses. Aleks broke into a jog, pushing past exhaustion and tired limbs. He scanned the surroundings for help. The city and its buildings and streets were too far away to provide shelter. The first Ravager made it through, screaming a charge. He and Henrik caught up to the others. Winded, Zorka was still catching her breath from her fall.

"Circle up," Aleks ordered, watching the dwarves fan out to surround them.

Everyone scrambled for positions, even beleaguered Zorka made an effort to get to her feet. She propped herself against the ground, teeth bared in a vicious snarl. Zaria took a protective stance, shifting in the group as Brunhild circled like a shark.

The lieutenant grinned maniacally, all forehead and hair, her helmet lost somewhere in the tunnel or cave. Her blonde, frizzy, and matted hair blew in the wind, tendrils streaming down her back. Roaring, she pulled out her sword, its emerald gem glinting cruelly.

"We have you surrounded," she crowed. "Hands up where we can see them, Princess."

Chapter Four: Brunhild Wins Her Prize

With resentment flashing in her purple eyes, Zaria complied, cautiously raising her hands in the air like a criminal before an officer of the law. Beside her, Aleks tensed. Out of the corner of his mouth he whispered, "Don't do it."

She huffed. "I'm not an idiot."

"I know," he soothed. "I'm just worried. You don't know what eyes may be watching or ears listening."

"Fritjof, you mean," she said. "It occurred to me, too. What if Brunhild and the Ravagers are under his control? They came through his passage."

"And they won't listen to reason," Filip whispered on the other side of her.

"None of you move," warned Brunhild. "We're going to tie you up."

Geirr grumbled, his blue eyes wary. "I am getting really tired of being tied up like a prized pig."

"I wish Airi was here," Christoffer said, pouting. "Where is your stupid bird?"

"I wish I knew," said Aleks, scanning the skies once more for signs of her.

The dwarves inched inward, closing in on the group. One withdrew a length of innocuous silver chain. At the sight of it, Zaria inhaled sharply, jerking her hands down. She shared a look of horror with Henrik to the side of her. His grim expression said he'd recognized the chain, too.

"What do you think you're doing?" Zaria demanded, facing Brunhild.

"Neutralizing a threat to Jerndor; starting with you. Hands up, Princess."

Filip and Aleks closed ranks in front of her, blocking the dwarf's path. "Don't come any closer," Filip said, steel hardening his words.

The chain, which appeared harmless in the morning light, was anything but. Of dwarvish origin, the chain was fashioned from a special ore found within the dwarf kingdom of Jerndor and forged in the fires of its sister state of Malmdor. The same ore could be found in the makeup of the Drakeland Sword and in the great mirrors that the dwarves used to transport objects and people vast distances.

In the mirrors, the ore facilitated fluidity and malleability, allowing users to slip into and out of them with ease. In the sword, it gave the weapon the strength to withstand dragon intimidation, allowing it to meet dragons in battle without fear. In the chain, the ore dampened magical output. Its creation, originally intended to stop dragons from using their powers of animal magnetism, now would stop Zaria from using her magic as well.

It was too distressing for words to lock up a sorceress with the very same material as one would a dragon from which she'd sworn to protect the world. Surely Aleks thought they would not be so cruel. A sorceress such as Zaria was good. She was not evil and did not deserve this fate. If her magic was drained, Fritjof would win. They couldn't let it happen. He'd rather

Zaria expose the true nature of her gifts to all and sundry than see her suffer.

"We have the sword," Henrik said, pitching his voice loud. Condemnation filled his words. "The Drakeland Sword cuts through the bonds of those chains. You cannot hold her."

"We'll take the sword, too, Stag Lord," said Brunhild, the sound of victory in her voice. "Don't you worry about that."

"We won't let you," Geirr said, narrowing his gaze and cracking his knuckles. "It's inhumane."

Henrik thrust out his jaw. "You talked of us breaking the Dragomir Treaty? Would you care to pitch the full fury and might of the ellefolken and elves against the dwarves?"

"Tree-hugging saps," Brunhild dismissed. "Besides, you don't speak for Silje."

"Maybe not," Henrik conceded. "But Queen Helena will never stand for it."

"Nor Niffleheim," declared Aleks, as the dwarves surged forward.

"Who's going to stop me?" Brunhild sneered. "You? You're nothing. You have no army, and I have you and your friends. It's over."

The Ravagers grabbed him and Filip. Aleks kicked and punched, throwing his elbows and knees everywhere he could reach. He broke noses. Beside him, Filip was a madman, gone berserk. He created space around him, as he fought with frenzy. But even with them going all out, and Henrik and the others at their backs fighting just as hard, the Ravagers slowly subdued them. Not even Zorka swayed the tide of the fight. Numbers simply weren't on their side. Dwarves piled on top of the troll until she was flattened on the ground under their combined weight.

Through it all, Zaria kept a steady gaze on Brunhild. She lifted neither a hand nor a finger in her defense. The Drakeland Sword strapped to her side, she looked as fierce as any Valkyrie of lore. Her eyes flashed with magic, but she stayed poised. She was a figure of calm in the raging storm around her.

"Fight back, Zar-Zar" Filip begged, as he was forced to his knees by two dwarves.

Aleks was forced to kneel next to him. "Do as he says," he entreated. "I was wrong. Show your gifts."

"Hush," said Zaria calmly. "It's going to be all right."

"How can you say that?" Henrik demanded. He'd been shorn of his golden antlered cloak. It lay bloodied in the dirt several meters away. "If you won't listen to them, listen to me. You can't be bound. Your magic –"

"Enough. Silence them. Permanently if you have to," Brunhild ordered. She snatched the chain from her subordinate and marched through the ranks, halting before Zaria. "Give me your hands."

"This is crazy!" Christoffer shouted, jerking an arm free. His guards wrestled him back into place, clocking him over the head for his troubles. Dazed, he stared in dread at Zaria as Brunhild grabbed her wrists and began wrapping the chain around them.

"Fritjof is real," Zaria said, quietly. "You're under his spell. The women under your command, you must love them. Why would you put them at risk?"

Brunhild snorted, twisting the chain tighter. "You'll say anything won't you. I knew you were a fake. You're the reason Prince Floki is locked up under house arrest. He doesn't believe you, and I don't either. How could you kill Koll? You are pathetic. You're nothing like your mother."

"Floki," growled Filip. "He's a goblin's arse."

"You can't trust anything Floki says," Zaria said, wincing as Brunhild jerked the chains. Her bronze skin paling as sweat beaded on her brow.

"I can't trust anything you say," Brunhild returned, checking Zaria as she stumbled. "I see the magic is already being drained from you. Good."

"This isn't right, guys. This isn't right. What do we do?" mumbled Geirr.

Agony seized Filip, emanating from his every pore, not for himself, but for Zaria. His skin flushed and paled moment by moment as he fought for control. Christoffer and Henrik renewed their struggles. Their guards bound their hands, one by one, even Aleks', and then looped ropes around their ankles so they couldn't move – an indignity nearly as bad as what befell Zorka. The Ravagers hogtied her, stringing her wrists and feet behind her, so she couldn't even wiggle.

She snarled, "I'll rip your spines out through your nostrils and make you wear them around your necks, you yellow-bellied cowards."

"Graphic," Aleks said appreciatively, while thinking highly unlikely given her current incapacitation.

Through it all, Zaria's breath grew shallower and shallower, until her eyes rolled up and she fainted. The scene seemed to unfold underwater. Aleks felt disconnected, as if he was witnessing the world from above himself. At a loss for what to do, all he could do was watch her fall. This couldn't be happening.

They were the good guys. Zaria couldn't be without magic. It wasn't right or fair. How could they stop Fritjof now?

Where was Airi? Where was his sister? Or Saskia? Where were the rest of the fey? Something had to have happened to them. Perhaps the dwarves had had inside help. How else would they have made it through the plains without a patrol finding them? Their march was so noisy, they could wake the dead.

Was their foe Grimkell, his birth father? Had he helped the Ravagers? Had he arranged for the fey's focus to be elsewhere? He wanted the throne badly enough to have orchestrated this. But that didn't make sense. Grimkell didn't want Aleks around. He had no reason to go after Zaria.

Brunhild ordered her warriors to lift Zaria and carry her away. They put her on their shoulders and began marching as if they had claimed a great prize.

That forced Aleks out of his thoughts. Jerking his head in the lieutenant's direction, he demanded, "Where are you taking her?"

"Jerndor, to my liege," said Brunhild. "He'll know what to do with her."

"Do you mean King Flein or Prince Floki?" snapped Henrik. "You have broken the Dragomir Treaty."

Her eyes flashed with hatred. "She broke it first."

"You'll be branded a traitor," Henrik warned. "They'll say you're in bed with dragons."

"Bite your tongue," she hissed.

"History will remember this day as the day the Ravagers lost their way," he sneered. "They'll say you're what went wrong with the dwarves."

Lashing out, she struck his temple, leaving a cut from her boot. "One more word from you and the ellefolken will be without a Stag Lord. What will your species do then? Mate with trees?"

Henrik pitched woozily to the side. Brunhild turned and stormed away, barking for her dwarves to head back into the plains. Aleks stared miserably after them, feeling the worst sort of failure. Beside him Filip was distraught. He'd turned to Geirr demanding the blue-eyed teen untie him. Geirr's dark fingers flashed against the white ropes, as he tugged and jerked on the knots. Christoffer propped Henrik up, the Stag Lord's blood pooling steadily between them.

The Ravagers disappeared through the tunnel, and Aleks, who hadn't realized he'd been holding his breath, expelled it on a harsh string of invectives, cursing everyone and everything. Geirr got Filip free, and the blond jumped to his feet. His fingers flew through the knots binding Geirr. Freed as well, the two turned their attentions on Zorka, struggling with her bindings.

Soon the sound of the Ravagers faded away. Hope deflated in Aleks' breast, and he slumped forward. A stubborn, frustrated tear streaked down his cheek, and he furiously rubbed it away on his sleeve. How were they going to get Zaria back now? What hope did he have of finding her? It hadn't even been a day and he was failing as a king... as a friend. Fritjof had won.

All hope lost, Aleks stared bleakly at the ground, his friends' words buzzing like bees in his ears, droning each other out. He couldn't make out a word they were saying. Christoffer grabbed his wrists and began untying them. His lips were moving, but Aleks didn't understand him.

Christoffer waved a hand in front of his nose, and he blinked. The oppressive weight on his chest grew heavier as the air grew denser. Energy began to crackle all around them, raising gooseflesh along his arms. It zinged almost painfully against his skin as it zipped around.

"This is for your own good," Christoffer said, the first words to penetrate the fog around his thoughts. Aleks blinked at him, confused. "Sorry, man." Then the dark-eyed teen slapped him across the cheek.

Raising a hand to block a second attempt, Aleks snapped, "I'm back. I'm back, okay?"

"Where did you go?" Christoffer asked, concern deepening his words. He jerked, slapping his arm. "Ouch. What is happening?"

A tendril of magic curled in the air, the first visible spark to light up the space around them. Zorka prodded its whizzing form with her finger. It zapped her. In alarm, she snatched back her hand, examining her finger for damage. Seeing none she harrumphed, sticking her hands under her armpits. Her tail twitched in irritation, as it batted more tendrils away from her.

More of them sprang to life, streaking like carnival lights from a tilt-a-whirl. Aleks watched them suspiciously, as they danced around the group. A veil seemed to drop out of nowhere, and suddenly the group was not alone. Surrounded once more, Aleks clutched Christoffer's shoulder in surprise. It took a minute for him to process that the faces before him were friends not foes. It wasn't the dwarves standing in front of him.

Looking equally shocked to see them, Airi, Nori, and Saskia stared agape. Saskia was too beautiful to bear. The sight of her instantly made him feel better, like the world hadn't just tilted full-out for destruction. Her short cropped white hair blew softly in the wind.

Their gazes locked, hers bluer than the deepest sapphire, and he raised a hand to wave, before dropping it, a sad smile tugging on his lips. Her pale pink lips stretched in an answering smile, revealing irresistible dimples.

"Hey, Red," she said affectionately.

Airi launched from the winter fairy's shoulder, drawing his attention. The white raven flew to him, landing with a sharp "Eye-riii!" The prick of her talons through his clothes grounded him, keeping him from dwelling on the negatives of their situation. She nipped at his ear, and he stroked her feathers.

"I deliver message," she cawed, piercing him with her icy blue eyes.

"You did," Aleks said, still trying to sort out how everyone he thought missing had appeared out of thin air.

He scrutinized his sister, looking for clues. One last bit of magic danced along Nori's outstretched fingertip. She snatched her hand back, curling it around her dress. She eyed Zorka briefly, wariness etched in her eyes, before facing Aleks once more.

"Baby brother," she said relieved, pulling him into a hug. "How on earth did you get here? Was that Zaria's magic that I touched?"

Behind her flowing red hair, he saw that all around in the fields foxes and fey were poised for attack. Most were aimed at the tunnel, but a few, who had felt the magic in the air had turned to see its source. They stared openly at him, causing his ears to redden.

He pulled back. "The Ravagers took Zaria."

She canted her head to the side. "Took her?"

"Ravagers in Niffleheim?" Saskia barked, surprised. She scanned the surroundings. "Where? No dwarf army is allowed in here. The Dragomir Treaty –"

Henrik stepped forward, glowering, his words soft and dark, "– is void concerning the dwarves. They put her in those chains. She fainted from the loss of her magic."

Nori's eyes grew as big as apples. "Why would they do that? She's the only one who can fight Fritjof!"

"That's just it, isn't it?" said Christoffer, placing his hands on his hips. "Fritjof is blinding them."

Filip whipped his head around. "They're in league with Floki. You heard Brunhild."

"Who's most likely in league with Fritjof," said Christoffer. "I mean look at the last time. The prince paired up with Olaf and tried to overthrow his dad."

"We have to rescue her," said Geirr.

"Understatement of the century," said Aleks, blowing out a harsh breath.

Filip looked ready to bolt to do just that; only Henrik's steadying hand on his arm stopped him. He caught the Stag Lord's eyes and said, "We should mount a rescue right now. We have the entire Autumn Court here."

"Agreed," said Henrik.

"Why didn't she rescue herself?" asked Zorka. "I can't be the only one thinking that. She has all this magic and just lets Brunhild march right up to her and put her in chains? Kanutte's right. She's not her mother's little princess."

"She did it to save us," said Aleks, around a lump in his throat. "She is Queen Helena's princess. Every inch. Nobody else could have done what she just did. She sacrificed herself."

Zorka grunted. "If you say so. From what I've learned about Helena though, she's no damsel."

"We were outnumbered," Geirr said, defending Zaria.

Aleks nodded. "She didn't want us hurt. If only we had known we were spitting distance from allies." He spun to glare at his sister. "Where was your truth power then?"

Nori sniffed. She jerked her head towards Christoffer. "It's as that boy said, dragons obscure it. Their very nature warps reality. Fritjof, he's growing more powerful, if he can blind me."

"My name's Christoffer, geez," he said, shaking his head. "How do you not know that?"

"It's not the first time Fritjof has clouded your vision," Geirr said, focusing on the matter at hand.

She held his gaze. "No, it is not," she acknowledged. "I recognized it too late, but at least when I finally did, I broke it."

"You rent the veil of the dragon's magic," Zorka said, scratching her nose and sounding impressed. She gestured vaguely at the air around her head. "It felt like the atmosphere before a storm. Crackling."

"My power seems to have a new facet," Nori said, raising her finger with no small hint of pride. "I've never done something like that before."

"That's great," Filip said, brusquely. "Now can we please go rescue Zaria?"

"Not so fast," said Saskia, flicking her wrist and creating an ice crystal in her hand. "We can't just march to Jerndor. The Thief of Peace's Passage will be closed. It's almost dawn."

Filip's green eyes gleamed with fire. "Then Brunhild and the others are trapped in Niffleheim. No way they'll make it back to the passage in time."

"Hold up," Nori said, holding her hands out. "It's more than the time. We have a colossal problem."

Zorka nodded. "How am I going to get back through the passage?" She pointed to the shattered creeper. "The rolling thingy is broke, and Zaria isn't here to conjure a new one. I'm stuck here until we get that sorted out."

"Not to mention these fey aren't soldiers," said Saskia, tipping her head in the direction of the throngs waiting and watching from the grass. "We were aiming for quantity when we rounded them up. We promised them they wouldn't have to fight. They're just a show of force."

"But they have powers," protested Filip. "They don't need formal experience to fight."

"Their powers aren't strong enough," said Nori. "They're commoners. Most of their magic is small, things to assist their day-to-day lives. It's their numbers you have to worry about."

"My father and I are among the exceptions," explained Saskia. "His power lies in strategy. If he knows all who are involved, the weapons, and the location, he can't lose a fight."

"That's rather unfair," said Zorka. "How do you beat him?"

"With the element of surprise," said Nori with a sniff. "Although you'd have to be pretty crafty to surprise Sivert. He thinks of everything."

"He's requested a meeting with you," explained Saskia, almost apologetically. "That's the colossal problem Nori's talking about."

Aleks, eyebrows pulled down, appeared puzzled. "Your father wanting to talk to me is the most troubling thing on your mind? And not Zaria being captured?"

She flashed him a rueful smile. "You don't know my father. He's um, ah —"

"Going to eat you alive," finished Nori. "If you want to rescue the sorceress, —"

"We do," said Filip and Henrik at once. The boys shared a troubled look and a truce seemed to form between them. They both wanted her back. Aleks, Christoffer, and Geirr, as well.

"As I was saying," she sniffed. "You'll need his help, which he might grant because of his daughter. That is, if you survive long enough to ask him for it."

"He's not that bad," said Saskia, glaring. With eyes wide, she turned her gaze on Aleks, and he found himself falling into their deep pools. His heart lurched uncomfortably, and he massaged his chest. She must've mistaken the gesture, because she added plaintively, "Really, he isn't nearly as bad as Nori is making him out to be."

Nori raised a sardonic eyebrow. "Except he is."

"You're toast," crowed Christoffer, attempting to inject levity, when none was to be had. "Toasty, toasty, Mc-Toastykins."

"Toast," agreed Airi, and that more than anything struck fear in Aleks' heart.

Chapter Five: The Fifth Fox Throne War

"I should talk to him," said Aleks, licking suddenly dry lips.

"I don't like it," said Henrik, with his hands on hips.

"I hate it," hissed Filip. "We should be rescuing Zaria, not running off to meet your girlfriend's dad."

"It's the only way," Aleks said, casting a plaintive look at Filip, hoping he'd understand. It was a feeling he couldn't describe, but he knew Zaria would be lost to them forever if he didn't talk to Sivert first.

"That's ridiculous," Filip snapped.

Aleks laid a hand on his shoulder. "We can't rescue Zaria without backup. We were beaten by them with her, we'll be slaughtered without her, and then nobody will rescue anybody."

Nori nodded, respect glittering in her brown-eyed gaze. "My little brother is right. We cannot pursue without proper backup. If he can get Winter to support him, he'd have half of the four courts backing his claim."

"You'd think we'd do something to rescue her," Christoffer said, crossing his arms. "Not just talk about it. If we don't help her now, we might never find her."

"I *am* doing something," said Aleks, clenching his fists. "I want to save her too, but she's safe for now."

"How do you figure?" asked Geirr.

Aleks looked his friends in the eye, one-by-one. "They chose to bind her. They could've killed her."

"We shouldn't be trusting dwarves under dragon influence to behave rationally," Henrik said. "They might kill her, still."

"Don't say that," said Filip, looking green in the gills. "I couldn't bear it."

"None of us could," said Aleks. He held out his hands in supplication. "We have to be smart, not rush in like fools without a plan."

Despite the driving urge to go and rescue Zaria, Aleks convinced the others to rein in the impulse. He thanked the fey who had answered Nori's call for help. They had done the crown a great service, and he wouldn't forget it. Most appeared flustered at his words; he chalked it up to nervousness, until Nori whispered in his ear that no other ruler had ever thanked their subjects before.

Red stained his cheeks. Where had common decency gone in Niffleheim? The shame of his birth family weighed heavily upon him like an anchor. There was so much to atone for and fix. It was daunting even to consider beginning such a task, but it could wait. It must wait until Fritjof had been dealt with.

He and the others followed Nori and Saskia to the Autumn Court, traipsing down the slope to the city by the inland sea. The wreckage of the Autumn Court smoked and smoldered around them. It had endured two coups back-to-back and hadn't yet had time to recover.

Buildings made of crystal lay in waste, holes smashed through their sides by magic and science. The war had been indiscriminate as two sides fought for supremacy. First his aunt and uncle waged war against his father, and then Aleks and his supporters went against his aunt and uncle. The court hadn't had a chance to breathe. The fight had been so desperate to those involved that breathing had been a luxury set aside. The outcome had been too precious to leave to chance.

A fine, gray dust coated everything, turning the city into an ugly industrial wintery landscape straight from a Dickens' novel. Figures moved, darting from place to place, each on a mission, each hoping to see a little progress made. Amazed at their transformation, Aleks stared, agog. He hadn't expected it.

Days ago, everyone had crept through on tenterhooks, casting furtive glances at every shadow, preparing to launch into a fight or to run from it at the slightest provocation. Today, the court was a bustling hive of activity. Fey dashed to and fro carrying tools, balancing baskets, and carting wheelbarrows full of crystal – broken remnants and freshly hewn blocks. Many worked together to clear the streets of the rubble of war and to repair their court.

Saskia saw his astonishment and grinned. "They have hope because of you."

"What have I done?" asked Aleks, squirming under her admiration. "What do I know of being king? Let's face it; my mom still does my laundry."

"It's no small thing that a changeling is king," she said gently, grabbing his hand. "A changeling has never been on the throne."

Nori huffed. "Just endorsed for one, and it didn't turn out well for any of them." Worry darkened her gaze, as she looked at him.

Alex grew quiet. The history lessons shared with him over the last several days detailing the series of Fox Throne Wars came sharply to his thought. He knew he should heed Nori's warning: a changeling may have been backed for the throne, but none had made it to coronation. His neck was on the line more than ever before. He'd be wise to protect it. Certainly Grimkell would want him to skip town before the big day.

The facts swam in his head like darting schools of fish, there one instant and gone the next. The first fairy to connect with the Lost Well had been a royal princess from the Spring Court. She'd ruled for a while under the guise of divine providence; then envy took hold of the Summer Court, as they sought to control the royal, because they could not control the well.

When she died without an heir, many strove to be next in the line of succession, seeking the power of the well. Nobles killed each other in an intemperate battle that ended in a tentative truce all four courts agreed to uphold. The courts would take turns, ruling one after the other consecutively. The chosen ruler had to be childless to ensure the proper and fair line of succession.

All was fine for a while, until King Jako of the Summer Court took the throne and forced his preteen children into exile as fey changelings in order to uphold the treaty. By many the move had been considered barbaric, by others as greedy. Nevertheless, King Jako's decision opened a way to the throne which those with children had thought closed to them.

After being assassinated by a Winter changeling, King Jako's children returned to Niffleheim, each seeking to claim the throne for themselves as his heirs. Every court backed a different changeling, except for Winter and Spring; but despite that, Autumn and Summer were united enough in their dislike of the third changeling to try to work together. In the end, despite their alliance, they couldn't put aside their own differences and desires, and Autumn eventually decamped, joining the other two courts and forcing Summer to surrender.

The treaty was revised again to suit the new ruler and further excluded any fairy with changelings from taking the throne. They did not want another debacle. It was agreed to re-exile King Jako's children. Not content, however, to live in the human world, and having a taste for power, they conspired together and laid in wait, seeking revenge.

When Autumn Court's Queen Effi got wind of their efforts to return, she passed a new, controversial law. Any fey, whether of human heritage (because they were stolen) or fey-born (because they were abandoned), would be marked on the back of the neck the instant they became a changeling. Fey changelings outside of Niffleheim, if they could be found, were to be forced to submit to the branding. This meant that even if fey changelings returned, they would be reduced to servitude at best, and slavery at worst, along with their human changeling counterparts, despite their magical powers and prowess.

Naturally, the changelings of both heritages revolted. Winter Court's changelings offered their services to Summer and Spring, and by their hands or perhaps by another court's hands, Queen Effi met the same fate as King Jako. The late Summer king's changeling children returned, but, as before, the courts couldn't decide who should take the throne.

Poison killed two of the changelings, while Spring beheaded the last of them. So ended King Jako's line, with none ever holding the power of the throne. The war might have continued, with the death toll rising as lawlessness spread, except that a Winter royal gained the well's allegiance, which settled the matter for a time.

New laws and treaties added more layers to the complicated politics of the fey. Humans no longer could be taken and turned into changelings, and a changeling could never rule over Niffleheim.

The fey changelings living with their Viking families, boiled at being cut off from their true lives and took their cue from the failed rebellion of King Jako's children, extending their aim. Not content to win just the throne itself, they pitted themselves against all full-blooded fey and the practice of creating changelings at all. The resulting war was the worst bloodshed the courts had ever seen, nearly extinguishing the four royal courts.

Only a secret deal between the Viking raiders and the generals of Summer and Winter saved the fey nobles and their lines. The Vikings withdrew, taking with them all changelings – human and fey – from the four courts. Summer then assumed the Fox Throne, to pass to Winter in a hundred years, an act that abolished the long upheld Four-Court Treaty. Niffleheim, freed of changeling influence, was then officially separated from the earth into a full-scale void with its only entrance to the human world contained within the Lost Well.

Spring and Autumn, the smallest of the courts, having suffered the most in the war, now were in the uncomfortable position of holding the fewest numbers in the savage political game. They were forced to serve the other two courts, a necessity in the minds of the Summer and Winter nobles, because they no longer had human changelings to serve them.

It was decreed that any changeling to return to Niffleheim would be killed on sight. This rule, so pernicious in the minds of the fey, was the norm for all changelings and many lives had been cut short. When Aleks appeared on the scene, only Zaria's quick thinking had saved him from a similar fate: first, when she wished for his safety and later, when she struck a deal with Grimkell.

Not honoring a bet was worse for a fairy's reputation than not upholding the law. Any fey whose word had no merit was deemed more worthless than a bottom-feeding ghoul – a fate deemed even more terrible than becoming a changeling. As a result, fairies were trained from infancy in the art of double-speak – implying one thing, but leaving wiggle room for various interpretations. Every fey held the ability to manipulate with words; it was no wonder that foxes in folklore were thought to be tricksters.

Knowing this, Aleks understood he had to be savvy. He again turned his attention to rescuing Zaria. The group wound its way through the court to the ruling seat, the Rød Skyttergraven. Aleks intent on persuading Saskia's father to form a war council, knew he would need an army to take on the Ravagers and save Zaria. If history tried to repeat itself, it might be the only way to keep his own head on his shoulders. That made earning Sivert's trust Aleks' top priority, even over and above his coronation and rescuing Zaria. Neither could happen without the first, and he was as absolutely certain of that as he was of his navigational powers — or at least when those were actually working.

As they approached, Aleks took in the sight of the great building. It was one of the few buildings still standing, and its imposing façade soared high. A ragtag group appeared to be cleaning it, leaving streaks of pure crystal shining through like fresh white paint under the dirt coating of a long unwashed automobile. Mangy foxes guarded the outside. Upon seeing him they hurried to transform and open the doors. Conscious of what his sister had said before, Aleks expressed his thanks, marveling that such a courtesy could garner tears in his subjects' eyes.

A fairy scurried over, dressed in garish livery decorated in large red and blue patches with black and white stripes. He bowed and extended a folded letter to Nori, before hesitating and shifting to offer it to Aleks instead. He took it and broke the seal.

"That's some outfit," Christoffer joked, raising a hand to cover his eyes. "It burns my retinas almost as badly as that troll stink bomb."

Nori sniffed in disdain. "You're looking at the colors of the Autumn Court. Show some respect."

"What, couldn't afford orange, could you?" asked Christoffer.

"These colors represent our heraldic crest," she said, pointing to tapestries that had been pinned on the opposing wall. "I had these pulled from storage. With Aleks as king we can display them again."

His eyes took in the image: two sitting red foxes ate black fish, their entrails spilling over a solid blue background. White and black stripes ran down the middle, separating the foxes from each other.

"Seems kind of gory," Christoffer observed.

Saskia flashed fangs. "You've seen nothing, yet. You should see the Winter Court's herald. It's a white fox covered in blood from chin to paws on a black and blue quadrant background."

"How do you know it's a white fox if it's covered in blood?" asked Christoffer.

Aleks folded the note, feeling grim. "Nori, have any of the other messengers returned?"

"None," she answered. "We haven't heard from anyone besides the Winter Court regarding your claim to the Lost Well and the Fox Throne, and they send Sivert, their general, as representative." Trepidation darkened her brow.

"That doesn't bode well," he said, handing her the note. "We may be mounting more than one rescue operation today."

She snapped the letter open and read, mouthing the words to herself. "Unacceptable," she hissed, shoving it toward Saskia.

The wintry fairy took it, sucking in a sharp breath as she read. "My father did what?!"

"He is holding our messengers hostage. All of them," Nori sneered.

Aleks squared his jaw. Through gritted teeth, he asked, "Do you think our messengers were caught before or after sharing the news about me?"

"Doubtful it was after," said Nori. "We're on our own. Just the way Carita wanted it. If we're not careful, she'll position herself first and take everything there is to take, including your throne and the Lost Well. This is not looking good for us."

"We have no support," Aleks said, scrubbing a hand across the back of his neck. "Even our own house is divided. With Ytorm, Cornelia, and their allies imprisoned there's no help from that quarter."

"We have fath —"

Aleks barked a bleak laugh. "Don't be naïve. You know Grimkell is looking for a way to get rid of me. He's probably worming his way into another alliance somewhere." If only he could have locked up Grimkell and Lukas, but they had supported the coup… to a degree, anyway, and deserved the chance to keep their freedom.

Nori bit her tongue. "You're right of course, but he has always favored his strongest offspring to be his tool. Why do you think Lukas and I always fought each other? We constantly had to prove which of us was better. You've proven you're the best. He won't do anything to you…"

"Yet," Saskia cautioned. "He'll watch and see."

Nori nodded. "He'll —"

"He's already colluded," Aleks interrupted. "Brunhild had to have had inside help. We can't trust him. I won't trust him."

"Perhaps," said Nori, uncertain.

"What are we going to do?" asked Geirr, as Nori turned to the servant and asked him to bring writing supplies.

Aleks stared at the note in Saskia's hands. "I will talk to Sivert. One-on-one, as he requests."

Saskia crumpled the note, anger staining her cheeks. "The hell you are. I'm going with you."

"Me too," croaked Airi, pecking his ear.

"Best not say anything, man," Geirr whispered to him. "You don't want two angry girls breathing down your neck. It's not worth it."

Aleks took his advice, keeping silent as Saskia paced, her short, white hair snapping back and forth with her abrupt turns. She tossed the note into a corner. "I can't believe him. I simply can't believe him."

"He used you," Henrik said, catching her eye. "Your father used you and took your news to spring this attack against Aleks and his crown."

Icicles formed in her hands. She gripped them, swearing, "I will gut him. I will slice him from belly to sternum."

"Pluck his eyes," added Airi.

"Good thinking," Saskia said, agreeing with the gory suggestion. "We'll take his tongue too. Lying to me, his only daughter, his only child. I'll show him. That measly no-good, rotten, –"

Aleks stayed her furious pacing. "Your loyalty is heartening, if bloodthirsty, but as Nori pointed out earlier, he has access to an army we need. We can use it to rescue Zaria. Plus, he's your father. I wouldn't want to come between you two."

She crossed her arms, pouting. "I'm going with you."

"But the note said –"

"I'm going with you," she said, her tone brooking no further argument.

Aleks smiled, feeling the pressure of his kingship lessen. With her beside him, he'd be able to navigate the deep waters ahead. "Thank you."

He shared a meaningful look with the girl before him. She deflated at the realization that he wasn't arguing with her. The icicles dispersed, melting away as she reached for his hands, gripping them tightly in her own. His heart raced at the coolness of her touch. Feeling it the thing to do, he raised one of hers and pressed a kiss to the back of it, the gallant gesture prompting Christoffer to make gagging sounds in the background.

Henrik tapped his chin. "It could be a trap."

"It probably is," said Filip, stuffing his hands in his pockets. "There's not much we can do about that."

Geirr's eyebrows knit together. "We should all go."

"If it is a trap, that would be unwise," said Aleks. "Some of us should stay behind in case another rescue operation is needed."

"At this rate, there'll be no one left who can rescue anyone," remarked Geirr drily.

The servant returned with the items Nori had requested. Snatching them up, she penned a furious note, melted a bit of wax, and pressed a seal to it. Handing the note to the servant she said, "Tell Sivert's messenger we agree to meet. The details are in the letter."

"Where are we meeting?" asked Aleks.

"At the site of the Firething," she said. At his raised eyebrows, she explained, "It's our assembly place, where all the influential members of the courts go for political and legislative purposes. It's neutral, and I'm hoping that will protect you."

"It's where the Four Court Treaty was written and signed," added Saskia.

"And where the Dragomir Treaty passed," Nori added.

Saskia cast a worried glance at him. "But safety isn't guaranteed. It's also the site of our coronations. The fifth war broke out there."

Nori rolled her eyes. "The circumstances demanded it. Summer and Winter were lucky it didn't happen sooner."

Saskia glared. "Spring and Autumn were lucky they haven't been wiped off the face of the void."

"We simply rebelled against unjust and unrepresentative rule," Nori hissed.

"You assassinated our king," Saskia said. "He would've been a great one. He had big plans."

"Not so great if we were able to nearly extinguish all the noble lines in his court and Summer's."

"Does this serve a point?" asked Aleks. "We have a meeting to reach."

"History always serves a point," Nori retorted. "This was the war that flipped the power balance back into Spring and Autumn's favor and was a coup to show that if you have raw power, numbers never matter.

"It's also the war that dictated dens couldn't have more than two kits, that whenever a third was born, one of them must be made a changeling and either killed or banished."

"I don't like that rule," Aleks said with a grimace. "I have a keen interest in living, so I propose we change that one right away."

Nori snorted. "The point, little brother, is that while you have little support and few backers, you are still powerful. You have the well, and you have your friends, Saskia, and me behind you."

The last still surprised him, not that he was foolish enough to say so aloud.

"Don't forget me!" piped up Airi, fluttering her wings indignantly.

"Never," he said fondly, stroking her soft feathery breast.

"Or me," said Zorka, tossing her long ears.

Aleks looked at her. "You're my friend, aren't you? You're one of us. You're already counted."

Zorka blinked in surprise. "I am?"

"Of course," he said, settling the matter.

"Sivert isn't going to know what hit him," Nori said. "He can't strategize his way around friendship."

A spark of hope ignited in him. As he looked at the determined faces around him, Aleks knew he couldn't fail. They wouldn't let him. He smiled widely, unknowingly showing fangs to the small gathered group, and missing the startled reaction from Geirr and Henrik. He did see Nori and Saskia exchange glances, but lost the chance to comment on it when Airi croaked, "Fox. Fox. Fox."

"Yes, Airi," he said. "We go to meet a sly old fox, and win him to our side."

She flapped her wings and launched herself overhead, crying, "Fox. Fox. Fox."

Chapter Six: Danegeld

Aleks' good feeling had long since left him. He stood with Saskia on his left, Nori on his right, and Airi on his shoulder, eyeing the entrance to the Firething – a pair of massive stones which looked like forgotten transformed giants. While shaped, the stones looked uncarved to his eyes. If he turned his head and squinted, he could almost imagine he saw facial features in the stone. Undoubtedly, a trick of the light.

Smaller stones outlined the field behind the megaliths forming a U-shape. These stones created a boundary and offered seats for rulers and nobles to perch, while dark wooden stands ringed the arena just behind them for others, most likely commoners, to take in the proceedings.

"No time like the present, I suppose," Aleks said, feeling decidedly unroyal as he made his way to the entry point. The giant stones had a way of humbling even the most prestigious of personages.

He wished he'd taken the initiative to ask Nori if there were traditional clothes for him to wear, something imposing, like Henrik's white cloak with golden antlers, to give him the confidence he needed. He'd have to make do with the bit of armor he was wearing and hope for the best, since he hadn't actually seen how it made him look in the mirror. He'd refused to wear the helmet, because far from bolstering him, it made him feel like a child playing dress up.

The man he was about to meet was not only a general of the vicious Winter Army, but also the father of the girl he liked. If he wasn't nervous about meeting the one, the other was sure to tie him up in knots. Would Sivert even take him seriously? He wasn't yet sixteen, *and* he was a changeling.

"Army," Airi warned, before making a repetitive knocking sound. Aleks petted her ruffled feathers into place. He had thought to see as much.

"I'm going to murder him," Saskia hissed softly, the air around her turning cold.

Aleks glanced down at her clenched fists, wrapped around long, wickedly sharp icicle daggers. He rested a hand against her pale, blue-veined wrist. "It's all right. You can put those away."

She shot him a disbelieving look. "It is not fine. He brought his whole contingent."

"He's missing the only one that matters," Aleks said meaningfully, clearing his throat. He dropped his hand, and she dropped her blades.

Looking at the figure on the far end of the field, he ignored his warming face. He attempted to smooth his hair down to cover his ears, and remembered too late that they had grown into a fully fledged fey set during the trials. His hair wasn't long enough to hide them anymore.

If that wasn't enough to deal with, Aleks had finally felt his new fangs after Airi had shouted 'fox' at him several more times. They unsettled him greatly, and made talking more difficult as he tried not to catch his words on them. Only his earlier practice while in his fox form kept him from sounding like a newborn babe, or a toddler lisping through missing teeth.

Aleks didn't like that his body kept changing rapidly and without his consent. It had been only a few days since the Lost Well had bonded with him, but that didn't seem to matter. He'd had a lifetime of practicing being human, and the Lost Well was blotting out his humanity as if his efforts had meant nothing. At this rate he wouldn't be able to recognize himself in the mirror. He felt like an imposter in his own skin. He missed control over his own body, his own fate...

Shoving those thoughts aside, Aleks focused on the task at hand, which was to convince Saskia's father to become his ally. The man in question, with long, wild white hair swept back in an array of loose braids along the sides of his face, stood near a pair of thrones made of crystal, watching him with an unwavering focus. Certain he'd seen and understood in these few moments more than Aleks had meant to reveal about his character and his feelings, Aleks' fought the urge to squirm.

"We should make our way to the thrones," said Nori.

As they approached, Aleks took in Sivert from head to toe. The man was as unrefined a fairy as Aleks had ever met. He and Krog, the head of the Hammer-Fisted Rock Smashers House, could be distant cousins with their matching heavy scars, squashed noses, thick necks, broad shoulders, and fists like hams. Aleks stopped there, thinking it unwise to link his girlfriend's father to a troll, even in his thoughts.

Sivert gazed at him from under heavily furrowed brows. "You're late," he noted, crossing his muscled arms and revealing lethal leather-wrapped knives. "The napping wolf does not get the ham."

"You brought an army, good," said Aleks, trying to sound like this made him happy, while ignoring the tardiness remark. He wasn't a schoolboy to be chastised. Not here. Not in this situation.

The whole Winter army wore gray wolves' pelts, and in anticipation of a fight, shifted from their spots in the stands. Aleks kept his gaze on the general and off the knives in his hands. He would not be intimidated. He would not show weakness in front of this skulk of salivating brutes.

After a long pause, Sivert said by way of explanation, "You have a sorceress in your pocket."

Aleks met Sivert's gaze, unflinchingly. No sense spilling that it was this same sorceress he needed to rescue. He cleared his throat. "It's good you're taking me seriously. I had wondered if you would."

Sivert scratched the long jagged scar cutting through his chin, bringing his knives back into focus. Aleks briefly noted that Saskia took after her father in this way, always using two blades, always calling attention to them. He hoped that Sivert would copy his daughter and not use them on him.

With his stern gray eyes boring holes into Aleks' head, the general grunted, "If you want Winter's support you'll have to pay danegeld."

Unable to conceal her incredulity, Saskia gasped. "Father, no. If he pays you once, it won't be enough. Ever. You'll keep pressing for more." To Aleks, she said, "Do not agree to this."

Airi snapped, "No danegeld."

"Think of it as… the price of peace," Sivert drawled, ignoring his daughter.

"You want me to pay protection money," Aleks said, seething. He would not be seen as a weak king. He would not give in to extortion. Trade, alliances, give and take, he could see, but to outright give to a determined taker? Not a good precedent to set.

The older fairy shrugged, the bone-white beads in his long tangled braids clinking together. "It doesn't have to be money. Think of it as… a bribe, a price –"

He nearly choked on his tongue as his eyes tried to pop out of his head. "Bride price? Doesn't she have a say? What if she doesn't like me? Can't we just date first? I won't force her to marry me."

Saskia waved her hands around in a panic. "No, Aleks, he didn't mean –"

"Bride. Bride. Bride," Airi tittered, laughing at him.

"Shut up, bird," Aleks growled, face flushing red.

"He said bribe, not bride," Nori cut in, annoyed and frustrated with his botched introduction to fey politics. This was not the impression they had been trying to make.

"Oh," said Aleks, blushing and fighting hard not to squirm at his mistake. Thank God, Christoffer wasn't here or he'd never live it down.

Roaring with laughter, Sivert pocketed his knives and slapped him across the back, nearly felling him where he stood. "I like you, son. May I call you son? That is an excellent danegeld to offer. I accept."

"Father," Saskia snarled, whipping out a fresh set of ice blades. "You will not force him to marry me. I'm a commoner, and not someone whose name can protect him. I'm not worthy, and you know it."

She had it backward, Aleks thought wildly, his heart pounding, still disbelieving the crazy scenario he'd gotten himself into with his careless words. New rule to be instituted immediately: never assume what someone says.

They weren't even sixteen, and her father thought marriage was a good idea? He wasn't adverse to the idea in the future – the far off future – when he was twenty-five – but now? He had to clear this up and fast, but first he had to correct her misperception, regardless of who was watching him, no matter how uncomfortable it made him.

He shrugged away from the general, and spun around to face her. After a slight bit of hesitation, he brushed a knuckle across her soft rosy cheek. Softly, he said, "I'm just a changeling. I'm nobody. You can too, protect me, just look at these hands and those blades. It's me who's not worthy."

Sivert grinned, the scar on his chin splitting in two. "See, the lad doesn't have to be forced. You'll do as I say. To think, you'll be a queen."

Airi bobbed her head. "Queen. Queen. Queen."

"Queen consort," Nori said, speaking up for the first time. Her face thinned as she bared her fangs. "She won't rule. Ever. Not even if Aleks dies. Nor will she ever learn the well's location."

"Who said anything about me dying?" Aleks asked, nonplussed. "That's something I'm trying to avoid."

Nori shook her head, exasperated. "Why else would Sivert want his daughter to be queen? With you out of the picture, suddenly he's in charge."

"Not if she's queen," said Aleks. "She'd be in charge."

"Nevertheless. Queen consort is all you'll offer."

Saskia jutted her chin at them. "You can't demand this of him or of me. I won't go through with it."

Aleks dropped his hand. He tried to curb the unexpected hurt flowing through him, but he understood. Even he knew it was much too soon for this talk. Just because he knew she was the one, – and yes, he understood it might be hard for others to believe – didn't mean she felt the same way.

"Dummy," Airi chirped, nipping at his ear.

He was such a dummy. He knew he was a bad risk. Being a king down here might sound great to some, but it was never anything he wanted. He didn't know the first thing about court life or ruling. He would be constantly under attack from all quarters.

Knowing all this, she might never say yes. In fact, she was right to say no, to protect herself from the danger that surrounded him, that would always surround him. She knew the dangers even better than he did, having lived in Niffleheim all her life.

He swallowed thickly, his Adam's apple bobbing, and turned back to Sivert, the better to hide his expression from her. "There you have it," he said, his voice wooden as he fought the urge to spew the bile climbing up his throat. "She doesn't want to marry me. Is there another danegeld you have in mind?"

"Dummy," Airi repeated.

Nori rolled her eyes. "Baby brother, you are obtuse. She doesn't want her father forcing the marriage. Saskia never said she wouldn't marry you."

His cooling face flushed crimson again. Clenching his fists, he stood still, trying to wrangle his out-of-control emotions and regain control of himself and the situation. This was not the time for self-reflection. This certainly wasn't the time for ham-fisted relationship discussions. He was a king now; he had to act like it.

A cool hand slipped around his own. He found his fist falling open to grasp Saskia's hand. He clung to it like a life line. She was it for him, and he knew that as surely as he once knew how to easily navigate anywhere his heart wanted to go. He searched for her feelings within her big blue eyes, too raw to protect his own.

"As you said," she said meekly, tucking a white strand of hair behind her ear. "We should – um, date first... although I don't know what that means."

"Kiss," commanded Airi, hopping up and down on his shoulder in agitation. "Kiss. Kiss. Kiss."

His ears burned redder, but he clasped Saskia's hand tighter. Steeling his resolve, he glared at Sivert, daring him to do or say something. "What do you want instead of a royal marriage?"

"Dummy," groused Airi, hopping off his shoulder and landing on Saskia's. She looked startled.

Sivert looked between his daughter, Aleks, and Airi, his growing grin, incendiary. He tapped his knife to his chin. "Only the head knows what lies within the heart; I can see which way the wind blows. You'll be marrying my daughter Saskia soon enough."

Aleks opened his mouth to protest that Saskia had a choice always, but she squeezed his hand hard, and he snapped it closed. Her touch left his skin feeling a little frostbitten, so he clasped her hand back, offering warmth and support.

Her father continued, "You're right to offer me a second choice. It's good to bribe your way into your sweetheart's father's favor. Why shouldn't I get two things out of our arrangement? Very well, I have it, you shall declare our house noble, give me a title, and an estate to rival Carita's family's home."

"You dare ask for more than one bribe?" Nori asked archly.

Sivert smirked. "I have a very large and very loyal army at my disposal, not to mention my skill with strategy, and a daughter your todd wants. A gift of three should be repaid with a like one, don't you agree?"

Nori turned toward Aleks. "We'd best look for a vixen bride for you elsewhere."

"I don't understand," Aleks said, looking between them. He knew Sivert referred to him when he said todd – the male counterpart to a vixen, but Nori's reasoning was lost to him.

She hissed, "Sivert can't be that powerful or command that much loyalty from his army. We should go."

Aleks looked askance at her. "But you said –"

Nori tossed her hair and sneered, "If he had as much control as he said, he could have staged a coup against Carita and taken the Winter court for himself, given himself a title, and settled into her family's home, as if it were his own."

"Watch what you say, vixen," Sivert growled.

He made a signal, and as one, the fey in the stands shifted, one moment relaxed and watchful, the next, on high alert with daggers in their eyes and sneers on their lips. Aleks glanced at their faces uneasily. Saskia bristled, and Airi ruffled. Their reactions warmed him and gave him courage. He cut his gaze back to Sivert.

The general growled, "If I don't like your answer, lad, you won't make it out of here alive."

There was only one real choice to make here. So he said, "I will give you the things you ask for and more —"

"Aleks!" cried Saskia.

"Baby brother!" shouted Nori.

"But let me make one thing clear," said Aleks. "This is not danegeld I am offering. It is an alliance. We will help each other. Walk with me, general, and I will discuss the terms."

Airi shuffled on Saskia's shoulder, as if preparing to take flight and join him on the walk. Aleks gave her a sharp look. "Stay with Saskia and my sister."

Her protest was sharp and to the point, "Eye-riii!"

The general signaled to his troops, and they dropped into insouciant, indolent poses. Aleks didn't like the looks a few of them were giving to the girls, but he decided to keep his mouth shut, at least for now, knowing they could handle it. Sivert joined him, and Aleks turned, leading the general along the field's perimeter. When they were out of earshot, Aleks cleared his throat.

"As you know, I did not grow up in Niffleheim."

Sivert snorted. "I'd be a fool not to recognize you as a changeling on sight, though you seem to be missing the mark of one."

His smile was grim. "Indeed. I'm told by the trolls I stink because of it."

"They're a barbaric, unsophisticated lot," Sivert said. "But their sense of smell is keener than any beast's."

Aleks thought that many fey had only the veneer of civility and were perhaps more barbaric than the trolls, but instead of saying that, he said, "Being king was not something I ever wanted. I do not have it in me to be a wily old fox like yourself. I am forthright and honest. I will trust you to be the same and a fey of his word."

"Ill advised," said Sivert. "How do you know I can be trusted? That I won't promise you everything you want to hear and then stab you in the back?"

"Because I like your daughter –"

"It's more than like, son," said Sivert.

Aleks looked over his shoulder, catching Saskia's concerned gaze. He returned his attention to her father. "Respectfully sir, I'm going to tell her first."

"You do realize that many fey trade on their families' very lives? That trusting a fey's word based on an oath against or for their kin is unwise."

He pondered that, knowing it was true, but instinctively knowing that he could trust Sivert to keep his daughter's best interests at heart. "My gut tells me she's more precious to you than any throne."

"If you say so," Sivert hedged, discomfited.

He probably wasn't used to being seen as a softie wrapped around his daughter's little finger. They were halfway down the field, far enough away from any prying ears He stopped, and turned to face Aleks, wanting to get to the crux of the matter.

"Down to business, son. What are the terms you're proposing for your alliance?"

"My support and aid to help not only yourself, but also your most trusted lieutenants achieve a higher status in Niffleheim. If this means giving you and them noble status, I will. If this means giving out estates, I will. If this means giving more power and wealth, I will. If it means giving you rule over the Winter Court as my right hand, so be it. I am at your disposal in such manner."

"In exchange for?"

"Your unwavering loyalty to my reign while I am king. I want your pledge that you will politic on my behalf for votes cast at Things should I need them. I want your army at my disposal. I want you to stop insurrections before they start. I want your absolute discretion in all matters large or small. That you'll never use anything I say against me, my friends, or my family. That you'll not harm those I hold dear, knowing that someday you may also be part of my family. In short, I want your full and total support for anything I want or need."

Sivert whistled. "That's a pretty hefty ask, lad."

"I'm offering a lot in exchange," he replied, calmly. "It's an offer you won't find elsewhere, because nobody else will value loyalty like I will."

Sivert scratched his chin with his scar. "Grapple with a pig, and you smell of his stink."

Aleks quirked an eyebrow. "I assume you're referring to the fact that I am a changeling."

"It'll be nearly impossible to help you politically. You're almost as sure as dead as soon as the other courts hear about you. I'm going to want more."

"What more is there to ask for?" Aleks asked, bewildered.

"I want the location of the Lost Well."

"Not a chance," Aleks said, flatly.

"Then I want you to give it to my daughter."

"Even if that means putting her in danger?"

"Yes," Sivert grunted.

"Then I want your word you won't coerce or trick her into sharing it with you or anyone else. Nor will you tell anyone that she knows the location."

"She can share it with me, if she chooses," he pressed.

"If she chooses."

Sivert grinned and held out his hand, "Son, you have yourself an alliance."

Aleks shook it firmly. "Great. Now I need your help rescuing my sorceress friend and stopping a dragon from escaping the Under Realm."

Sivert's grin slipped off his face, like he'd been hit with a bat. "I should have asked for the throne."

Chapter Seven: The Well's Gift

"I might have given it to you," joked Aleks.

"First lesson, son, don't say that down here again. Not ever," Sivert growled, the scar on his chin rippling in anger. "This is serious. Your life. My daughter's. Mine. Your friends'. Your sister's. It all depends on what happens next."

Aleks's face fell and he swallowed. "I am aware."

"Where's your sorceress?" Sivert asked briskly. He rested his hands on the knife pommels at his belt. "You said this is a rescue mission."

Aleks nodded and crossed his arms. "The Ravagers took her, and if they didn't make it to the Thief of Peace's Passage before daybreak, then they're hiding somewhere in the plains. Not that there are many places to hide, but we can't face them again without numbers."

"Dwarves," sneered Sivert. "I might have known. They've been plaguing us all summer long because of that aunt of yours and her foolhardy husband. This, though, is beyond the pale. They've left the passage, you say?"

"Yes, and came across the plains and through the tunnel into the clearing near the Autumn Court. They attacked us and bound Zaria in chains designed to stop dragons."

Sivert swore, running a hand through his long, white hair. "They've certainly escalated this. I hadn't realized it'd gone so far."

"It's the dragon and his machinations," explained Aleks. "He's almost certainly working with Prince Floki, somehow. Brunhild, their leader, said as much to me earlier."

Sivert's tactical mind was fully employed by the situation. "You'll need to form a swift rebuttal. A strong ruler is a respected one."

"I'll let King Flein handle his people. I can send him a message. For now, it's more important to get my friend back."

"Your white raven can do the job," said Sivert. "She's the only one who'll be able to get it delivered through their blockade, and she'll be the only one they'd trust to let into Jerndor. Is she okay with being blinded? They might want to cover her face so she can't report back to you their numbers and positions."

"Er...," hedged Aleks. "I don't know. I can ask her."

He rubbed his chin. "You're hopeful that the Ravagers haven't made it into the Thief of Peace's Passage, right? They may be hiding, waiting for the way to open. It is best to search while the trail is new. I'll get my scouts on it."

Together they turned back toward the thrones, where the others waited. Aleks gave Saskia a small grin and a thumbs up. Airi took note and her repetitive knocking sounds stopped. He hadn't been aware she was making them until the field went silent. His sister's rigid stance relaxed.

"This Brunhild was leading them, you say? Were they using their famous barbed spears?" Sivert asked. "What were their numbers?"

"Yes to both questions, and she came with thirty to forty of her best friends."

"That's better than the scurrying rats we've seen down here before. At least those ladies know how to have a good time. My soldiers and I love a good fight," said Sivert, anticipation glittering in his eyes.

Aleks gave him a wry smile. "Saskia likes one, too. What's the state of the other courts? How are they doing? When I was completing the trials, I saw other courts go up in smoke and flames. Which ones were they?"

"Summer," grinned Sivert, setting his scar off again. "I launched the attack."

"Why?" asked Aleks, dumbfounded.

"Because they were in league with Autumn," he answered. "I didn't like it. When courts start allying, it spells trouble for the others. Carita agreed with me, and with her blessing, I launched the initiative."

"And the other court? What happened there?"

Sivert shrugged. "To Spring? No idea. I didn't have a tail in that fight."

"You have a tail?" Aleks asked, momentarily distracted.

Sivert looked at him sideways. "Only when I'm a fox, son. It's a troll expression."

Aleks nodded and kept moving. "The infighting needs to stop. This is the sort of chaos that feeds into Fritjof's power. The more united we can be, the less of a foothold he has on Niffleheim," said Aleks, with absolute certainty.

Sivert grunted. "Fritjof is the dragon? Never heard of him. Are you sure you have your facts straight?"

"Do you know Nori's ability?"

"She can't be lied to," he answered, eyeing the redhead across the field. They were almost back to where they had started.

"Nori's ability is discerning the truth," Aleks agreed. "She came to warn me he was here, and just like you, I had no recollection of him. Fritjof's erased any memory of him from everyone's minds, and we have no idea how he's done it. Mentioning him by name cuts off all forms of communication unless you're standing in front of the person to whom you're talking. We had proof of him late last night, early this morning. He appeared in the Thief of Peace's Passage."

Sivert halted Aleks by placing a hand on his shoulder. "You're saying the dragon was in the passage? Should you have mentioned this to me first?"

"Zaria destroyed Koll," Aleks said. "If we have any chance of killing or containing Fritjof, it is with her. That's why we have to stop the Ravagers."

"Hold on. You're telling me that your little sorceress killed a dragon, an impossible task, but got caught by a measly forty Ravagers?"

Aleks sighed. "I know how it sounds, but it's a lot different fighting one dragon versus fighting a group of dwarves you think have been manipulated and are being controlled against their will.

"Zaria didn't want to hurt the Ravagers. She wants to free them from the dragon's influence, just as Olaf was freed from Koll's power by his death. When Olaf came to his senses, he was a changed troll, and changed for the better. She hopes the Ravagers will be the same."

"Sometimes you have to make the hard choices," Sivert said. "Innocents will be lost."

Aleks frowned. "That is not something she would agree with, and I don't know that I can agree with it either. Innocents should be protected."

"Even if they're acting out against those who would seek to help them?"

"Even so," Aleks said. "If someone's drowning, you help, even if they might cause you to drown, too. So it's best you do it safely."

"That's why you slug them in the head," Sivert groused.

"Knocking unconscious is not the same as killing," Aleks reminded.

"Son, you're making my job a lot harder with those words. Remember, it's a severed head which no longer plots."

Aleks laughed. "Take comfort in knowing that you'll be foiling a dragon's best-laid plans by seeking peace first."

"Let's not be too hasty," Sivert said raising his hands. "Don't tie up my options. I am the best strategist you'll find in Niffleheim, but even I can't pull off miracles. Some Ravagers may be hurt."

"No deaths," warned Aleks. "Zaria's sacrifice should be honored as best as we can."

"There may be one or two," Sivert hedged. At Aleks' burning glare he heaved a put-upon sigh. "I'll do my best to avoid it and tell my troops the same, but if it comes down to saving your sorceress or saving one of the dwarves, what would you have me do?"

"Save Zaria," Aleks answered with zero hesitation.

By now they had reached the girls, and Airi, unable to wait a moment more, flew to his shoulder. She sidled in closer, nearly brushing his ear with her feathers. The imminent anticipated touch caused gooseflesh to erupt on his neck. He nudged her gently away.

"Ease up, Airi. It's all right," he said.

"Everything good, little brother?" asked Nori. "I don't like that you went off alone to deal with him. He's a cunning fox."

"What were the details of your agreement with my father?" asked Saskia. She shot the general a glare. "If you don't like the terms, Aleks, you can break them. After all, you're the king."

"That wouldn't set a very good precedent, now would it?" Aleks teased. "It's all right. Our agreement is mutually beneficial."

"Eckart, Emrik, new orders," barked Sivert.

The rows of soldiers snapped to attention, even though only two were called. They stepped forward and made their way down the stands, where they stopped in front of Sivert like a pair of identical bookends. Aleks couldn't tell them apart.

The twins wore their hair long and braided like Sivert with silver beads threaded. Broad of shoulder and chest, with clean straight noses and deep sapphire eyes, they immediately made Aleks feel scrawny and inferior. He cast a sidelong look toward Saskia, wondering what she thought of them.

"Scout the plains. We're looking for Ravagers and their hostage – a girl. Report back when you've found both. Memorize everything. Don't forget a single detail."

Two sets of eyes widened slightly, surprised at the news, but otherwise their faces remained impassive. The fey sounded off and sloped away across the field. Aleks watched them go, before turning back to Sivert and the others.

"You'll let our messengers go?" Nori asked.

"Of course," said Sivert, then turning aside, he commanded a trio of silver-haired fey, "Free them."

The fey pulled out long wicked daggers and turned, revealing a trio of bound and gagged Autumn fey. Their bonds were sliced and the gags removed. Their guards lifted them up and dusted off their shoulders and backs. The Autumn fey, leery of the contact, jumped away. The Winter fey behind them pushed them ahead, and they scampered forward in alarm.

"It's okay," said Aleks, catching them. "You're safe."

"My liege," said the elder, a man with gray at his temples, whose name Aleks had forgotten already. "What are your orders?"

Aleks looked at the two women with him and back at the man. "Can you still deliver your messages to the other courts?"

"I can deliver them," he said. "Perhaps the ladies should return to court?"

The women gathered themselves together and tossed off the look of fear. With resolve and steel, one said, "I shall deliver my message, my liege."

"I as well," said the other.

At the look of determination in their eyes, Aleks nodded. "Very well. Go quickly, and let the other courts know there's a new king and that they are to send representatives to the Autumn Court."

They left the same way as had the twins. Aleks lifted a hand to Airi and she climbed up onto it. He brought her before him. "I have a special message for you, my girl. Do you think you're up for the task?"

She squawked indignantly at the suggestion, causing him to chuckle. "'Atta girl," he said. "Let's return to Autumn Court, and I'll explain. Sivert."

The general nodded in farewell. He shook hands with Aleks again, his hand swallowing Aleks'. He turned to his daughter and held out his arms. Saskia hesitated a moment and then lunged forward, hugging her father tight around the middle. He grunted and patted her back, before putting her aside and chucking her under the chin. The tender moment evaporated in a blink of the eye, as Sivert barked orders to his waiting soldiers.

Aleks held out his hand to Saskia, which she took. He laced their fingers together – both cool and warm. Nori fell into step on the other side of him, her fiery red hair blowing back, as if an invisible wind trailed its fingers through it. She seemed to want to say something, but held her tongue until after they had left the Firething. When they passed through the great entrance stones, she could no longer hold back.

In a fierce whisper she demanded, "What did you promise him?"

He cast her a sidelong look. "Everything he wanted in exchange for everything I wanted."

Nori looked nonplussed. "Baby brother, you didn't."

"I did," he confirmed. "We're asking him to rescue Zaria and help fight a dragon. It deserves a big reward."

"It's stupid," Nori insisted. She tapped her temple meaningfully. "He would have joined you for less."

"But why make him feel bitter once he learned the whole truth?" Aleks shook his head. "It was right to offer what I did."

"He didn't pressure you for marriage or the Lost Well's location, did he?" asked Saskia.

He squeezed her hand. "We reached a fair bargain that still leaves you choices."

She rolled her eyes. "What about *your* choice?"

"I've made it," he said, thinking of both the crown and the girl.

"Fox," agreed Airi in his ear. Then she added, "Message?"

He nodded. "Yes, you and I need to go to the Lost Well."

"That's dangerous," hissed Saskia. "You don't know where the Ravagers are in the plains. We should go back and ask my father for backup."

Aleks shook his head. "Your father and his people are not to know the location of the Lost Well."

"Then I'm coming with you," she insisted.

"Yes, one day, but not today," he told her.

She growled, "It's not safe."

He grinned at her as her hand in his cooled rapidly at her words. "If I sleep, the well will bring me back to it. Airi knows how to find me. She'll meet me there."

"How will you return?" she pressed, yanking her hand from his and placing it on her hip.

Nori frowned. "Must you go to the well to send your message? Is your message to someone on the surface? Who do you have to contact?"

"King Flein," answered Aleks. "It's too dangerous for Airi to deliver the message through the passage, and besides, we don't have the luxury of time to wait for it to open."

"I don't like it," said Nori.

"Me either," agreed Saskia, waving an icicle. "Wait until my father takes care of the Ravagers. Then you won't need to send Airi at all."

"It's not optional, I'm afraid," he said apologetically, just as they reached the outskirts of the Autumn Court. He knew if he were in King Flein's shoes, he'd want to be informed of possible rogue agents within his court. He nudged Saskia. "You two return to the Rød Skyttergraven. I'll be back before you know it."

"What are you going to do?" Saskia huffed. "Fall asleep here? You're coming with us."

"Well," Airi announced. "I go."

"I'll meet you there shortly," Aleks said, and then allowed himself to be herded toward the palace.

Inside, they regrouped with his friends, where he detailed the plans. Nobody liked it, but Henrik thought he and Saskia could scout the way and meet with him on his way out. Aleks agreed to this plan, so long as they took extreme care crossing the plains.

He departed to a large bedchamber in their suite of rooms. The four-poster bed beckoned. Piled in old, warm furs, soft and supple to the touch, Aleks had no trouble falling asleep. He burrowed himself into them, making a nest, and hunkered down, closing his eyes and letting his body relax.

Snug and warm, Aleks resisted Airi's insistent call, but the now familiar sensation of metal digging into his side, woke him up. Immediately, he missed the bed and rued his sleepless fate. With a yawn, he stood and Airi swooped over, landing on his outstretched forearm.

"Message," she prompted.

"Tell King Flein of Jerndor that there's a new king in Niffleheim. Let him know that he can't trust the Ravagers because they are working for his son Prince Floki, and Prince Floki, in turn, is either under the influence of the dragon Fritjof or working for him by choice. He must recall the Ravagers immediately and release Zaria. Niffleheim doesn't want a war with the dwarves."

She pecked at his hand. "No."

Incredulous, Aleks repeated, "No?"

"No," she confirmed.

"Why not?" he demanded.

She hopped up and down. "Too long. Too long."

"What are you, Twitter? Do I have a character count limit, too, or just a word count?" She stared at him with one icy eye, not deigning to answer that. He huffed. "Fine. Tell King Flein that King Aleks wishes to arrange a cease fire and to call off his Ravagers."

"King Aleks. Cease fire. Call off Ravagers."

"Precisely," he said, as she nibbled at his knuckle. He looked up to the opening in the well, judging that there wasn't much time left before the way closed.

Tossing her skyward, Aleks watched as she wheeled around the well once, twice, circling higher and higher. She drew even with the edge and landed, her majestic white wings folding back. From this distance and in the shadow of the rooftop covering he could barely see her. She cocked her head at him, as if questioning whether she should stay.

He waved at her. "Hurry back and be safe."

She took off in a flurry of feathers, screeching, "Eye-riii!"

Gone from his sight, Aleks lowered his hand and looked around him. There had to be a way to hold off waking up each day in the well. It was so impractical. Spinning around on his heel, he surveyed the piles of coins and goods littered at his feet.

"What do you suggest?" he asked aloud.

The silence continued unabated. Aleks stuffed his hands in his pockets, scuffing his shoe. He hadn't expected an answer. Not really, but somehow, someway, the Lost Well had chosen to bond with him. There had to be a way to communicate with it.

He felt a coin in his pocket and withdrew it. Tossing it away to a distant pile he said, "I wish there was a way to come and go as I pleased. It wouldn't hurt either to have these coins be less clingy. Why am I finding them in the oddest places all the time?"

A flash of red in his peripheral caught his attention. He turned and saw a black box appear in the hollow in which he'd woken earlier. His strides ate up the distance, and in seconds he was kneeling before the box. It was smooth, like glass. On the lid, an etched white raven created a stunning motif. Cautiously, as if it would bite him, he pried open the lid.

Inside nestled a black leather cuff with the same design. He picked it up to examine and a piece of paper fluttered down. Catching it, Aleks quickly unfolded and smoothed it out. It was covered in runes. He watched as they shifted and shimmered in the light, reforming into something he could read.

For your eyes only, destroy this soon.

Commit to heart, by rote learn.

Wear to be immune.

Take off to return.

You must visit at least once a moon,

Or waking here will be your least concern.

In addition, gather the coins that are strewn,

And wish on them for what you yearn.

What help I can be is your boon,

Whether or not you will discern,

That in this room your wishes will be most attune.

A wise king would not this gift spurn.

Or he may be like a mighty oak hewn,

Try it now and wish this note to burn.

That explained Zorka's appearance, he thought, and the box. For the first time, Aleks reached for the coins at his feet and plucked one up. He closed it in his fist and made the wish. In a flash, red fire licked up the paper. Brushing his hands, he scattered the ashes.

Excitement stirred in him; for once, he saw the well as a friend and not an enemy. What was the extent of the well's power? What could he wish for? If the well could bring Zorka to his side all the way from Trolgar, could it also bring Zaria? Could it fell a dragon? Could it stop a war? He'd have to find out.

Eagerly donning the cuff, Aleks scooped coins into the black box and secured the lid. He stuffed a few more in his pockets. He would not waste the well's gift. Tucking the box under his arm, he strode to the exit tunnel and slipped out, feeling in his gut that everything would finally turn out all right.

Chapter Eight: The Sixth Fox Throne War

Aleks fingered the coin in his pocket. He was in the corridor, thinking again about Zaria, and he couldn't wait. He made the wish and tossed the coin back into the well, not really confident it would work, but desperate to try. To his amazement, a wall of flame erupted and Zaria appeared, wrapped in chains.

Zaria, however, wasn't the only one to appear, putting a kink in his improvised plans. A pair of Ravagers propped her up between them, forming an unlikely pair of bookends. They seemed to be dragging her somewhere. They startled at seeing him.

"Oh, cra –"

"Get him!" snarled one. She pulled an axe from her belt and charged.

Aleks scrambled away, falling backwards against the wall in his haste. The black box fell to his feet and scattered its contents in a pool of silver and gold. He ducked as the axe whistled through the air and slammed into the rock, sending sparks raining down upon their shoulders. The other dwarf tried to jab him in the chest with a spear, and he just barely managed to roll away in time.

He looked over to see Zaria slumped on the ground. His heart squeezed in distress at her closed eyes. Her braided crown was lopsided and half fallen down. It clung to her cheeks for her face glimmered with sweat. She lay still as death. Peering closely, he was relieved to see that she took shallow breaths.

His focus on Zaria, Aleks almost took an axe to the face. He jumped out of reach, sending more coins flying as they spilled from his pockets. They clinked against the walls and bounced along the floors. Watching them scatter, he wondered if he should've kept to his original plan to leave magical solutions behind. What good was an empty pocket when a spear-wielding dwarf lunged toward him, forcing him to dodge yet again? He couldn't rely on something as fickle as a coin. He had to trust himself. He, not a coin, was Zaria's only hope.

After another set of their multipronged attacks, Aleks rued the fact that he hadn't gone to sleep in the armor Zorka had pulled from the well. He should have learned his lesson from the earlier encounter at the Firething and dressed for the occasion. He could really go for a weapon right about now. Not his bow and arrows, though; they wouldn't do him much good in such close quarters.

The next time the Ravager thrust her spear at him, he grappled for the weapon. He used his size and strength to haul her off her feet. She hung on like a limpet, and he couldn't loosen her grip. From his peripheral he saw the axe-lady swing at him.

He parried her attack, but with the clinging dwarf making every move cumbersome, he was forced to drop his hold on the spear to escape axe-lady's next attack. She came at him like a berserker, flashing metal and bony limbs everywhere.

She knocked his head with the side of the axe, stunning him. Dazed, he shoved her off, throwing her into the other Ravager. Then, rolling away, he suddenly found himself closer to Zaria, arresting him mid-motion.

Her violet eyes were open. She stared at him, eyes dull and dilated with pain. One trembling hand flopped in his direction. Her mouth shaped words he couldn't hear over the ringing in his ears. Probably "Duck,

Aleks!" as a thin feeble streak of magic left her fingers and slipped passed him.

Feeble though it was it still packed a punch. He turned his head in time to catch sight of magic knocking the spear-carrying Ravager off her feet, as it collided with her breastplate. She flew back and landed hard against the wall, before crashing to the floor in a heap.

One Ravager down; one to go. Finding axe-lady, Aleks climbed to his feet and stood warily in front of Zaria, bare hands outstretched to protect her. The dwarf glowered at him, her squinty eyes filled with unfounded hate.

Beside him the well's entrance shimmered and winked out, closing off any chance of escape that way. Loss of the golden light cast the corridor in deepening shadows. In the gloom that followed Aleks saw it – a flash of yellow in the dwarf's eyes – and it caused his heart to race. She was possessed by the dragon. She was Fritjof's creature through and through.

This unexpected twist was not good. Manipulation was one thing, but full control of another? That scared Aleks' spitless. He tried to swallow, but couldn't get past the lump in his throat. There had to be a way out of this. Perhaps he'd been hasty to dismiss the well's help out of hand. If he could wish the dragon killed, or even wish for a weapon, they might have a chance. Slowly, he reached for his pocket.

"Keep your hands up, Changeling," the Ravager barked. Gleaming sulfuric eyes tracked his every move.

He stood, holding them akimbo to show he had nothing in them. "I demand to talk to King Flein."

"I don't serve King Flein," she snarled. "I don't serve anyone, you pathetic little runt."

He laughed humorlessly. "I know who you really serve. You'd be better off serving a hag."

"Bite your tongue," she hissed.

"Aleks," Zaria said weakly. "Fritjof."

"I know," he assured her. "Save your strength."

"She's done for," the dwarf said with gleeful prediction. "She's no ellefolken princeling. She'll die soon. So much magic drained. So little strength left."

"Zaria is stronger than you know," growled Aleks, ignoring the fear that tried to swallow him whole.

The sickly grin on the dwarf's leering face slipped. "Enough talk. It's time for you to die, Changeling."

Lashing out, the Ravager attacked with all her strength. Her axe slammed into the rock where Aleks' had been standing moments before, cracking stone. She growled trying to wrench it free. He kicked at her legs, toppling her to the ground.

Grunting and swearing, Aleks wrestled her to the floor, using the axe handle to press against her windpipe. She spat at him, and he reared back. With a snarl the Ravager forced him off, sending the axe flying into the dark. It landed with a loud clank somewhere in the distance.

"Do you hear that?" shouted Henrik, his voice echoing back through the dark from somewhere far away.

"That's got to be Aleks!" cried Saskia.

Relieved, Aleks expected his foe to seek out her weapon and disappear. But she ignored the shouts and came after him instead, snarling in rage. Unprepared, he caught her blows with his stomach. The air expelled from his lungs in a whoosh. Struggling under the assault, he tried to bring his arms and legs up to block.

Then suddenly she was ripped away from him. Aleks caught a glimpse of antlers and a white cloak as Henrik put the dwarf on the defensive. She blocked his sword with the metal braces on her arms, but the force of his blows drove her back and back.

Saskia was right there in the mix, hurling icicle daggers. They shattered against the dwarf's metal breastplate. Each impact caused the Ravager to flinch as shards flew toward her face and stung her skin.

"Watch out," Aleks warned. "She's possessed by Fritjof. He's giving her some of his strength."

"All the more reason to end her," snarled Saskia.

The dwarf's foot brushed against something on the ground. With a shout of excitement, she dove for it. With the missing axe in hand she let loose a feral cry and grappled with Henrik and Saskia with renewed vigor. They grunted from the exertion to subdue her.

"Don't," whispered Zaria, struggling to sit up.

Aleks was by her side in an instant, helping her keep her balance. The chains around her body glowed a faint purple as they sapped more of her magic from her. She clutched at his shirt, pulling him to her.

"What is it Zaria?" he asked, leaning closer.

Her eyes darted around wildly before focusing on him again. "She's innocent," she said.

Saskia was thrown back with inhuman strength. She landed nearby in a tangle of limbs, claiming his and Zaria's attention. With a snort and a quick hair toss, the winter fairy bounded to her feet, forming new icicles.

"With all due respect, Princess," she huffed, hurling them at the Ravager before turning to look at them. "That is the stupidest thing I've ever heard. We're not playing kettupeli after supper here. We're brawling to the death. We take her out now before she gets one of us. It's the only play."

"No," Zaria said frantically. "He'll just possess another."

Aleks eased her grip on his shirt. He soothed, "So we knock her out."

Zaria shook her head. "Don't. He'll do the same."

"You're making things rather difficult, Princess," Saskia huffed angrily, parroting what her father had said earlier to Aleks. She parried another blow, protecting Henrik with the same move.

"We have to subdue her," Henrik said, jerking his antlers off his head.

"A good hit to the head should do that," muttered Saskia darkly, as the Ravager bodychecked her into the wall.

"You heard Zaria," Henrik said, shrugging the rest of the way out of his cloak. "Don't knock her out."

At Henrik's words, Zaria collapsed in Aleks' arms. What fight was in her slipped away as she lolled against him. Hugging her close, he chuffed her arm, before gently laying her aside. He stood, weaponless, but if they could get the axe away from the dwarf, he could help force her into submission.

Henrik positioned himself beside him to regroup, as Saskia launched a series of ice-blades at the dwarf. The Stag Lord had blood dripping from the corner of his mouth and a cut under his eye, but on his face he wore determination made of steel.

"Here," he said, handing Aleks his sword.

In the next breath, he charged the dwarf and grabbed at the axe with two hands. The wild confrontation escalated as the two grunted and grappled in the tight space. With a wrenching two-handed heave, Henrik wrested the weapon from the rabid Ravager.

She cried out bitterly and tried to bite his hand, but Aleks swooped in and laid the blade at her throat. "Don't move," he warned.

The glowing yellow eyes regarded him with menace. Blood dripped from a thin line as the dwarf pushed herself forward into the sword. Aghast, Aleks almost pulled the sword away, unable to believe his eyes at the willful self-destruction, but a warning growl from Saskia stayed him. He held firm as she and Henrik set to work.

The Stag Lord yanked the dwarf's arms behind her while Saskia tore off Aleks' shoelaces and handed them to Henrik. Only when they bound her tightly did Aleks drop the sword from the woman's neck. She hissed at him like a snake.

A moan filled the passage, and Aleks looked toward Zaria, thinking she was the source. The girl was out cold. The moan came again, and he remembered the other Ravager. Saskia found her and yanked her up by her leather armor vest. The dwarf cradled her head and gazed at them in bleary confusion.

"What's going on? Why do you have Hertha tied up like a prized pig?"

"You attacked us," Aleks informed her just as the possessed Hertha shouted, "They ambushed us!"

"I don't remember," the confused dwarf said staring back and forth. She saw her spear and made a move toward it.

Saskia pointed a glistening ice dagger at her. "I wouldn't take another step, if I were you."

"I think you were possessed, which is why you don't remember," said Henrik as he bent to gather his cloak. Instead of putting it on, he laid it across Zaria's prostrate form. She shivered and curled two fingers into it, clinging for warmth. He touched her cheek, "It'll be all right. Hang in there a little longer."

She sighed, and Aleks handed him back his sword. He looked at the unknown dwarf. "Your friend, Hertha, is now in the throes of your recent predicament."

"Possessed?" the dwarf said, disbelief coloring her words. "Only a dragon can possess someone and they're all locked up in the Under Realm."

"Take a closer look at Hertha," invited Henrik as he cleaned the blood off the blade against his pant leg. "You'll see it. The eyes are unmistakable."

"Hertha, look at me," she demanded, fear in her voice. Hertha gazed coolly at the Ravager, causing the other to gasp. "You've never looked at me like that. We're best friends."

"If we're best friends, why haven't you attacked these children and freed me?"

The dwarf trembled. "What's my name, Hertha?"

"What an insipid question," Hertha sneered, yellow beginning to glitter in her irises.

"I'll ask again. What is my name?"

Hertha fumed. "I'm not going to deign to answer that. We've been friends for ages, but these children say a few words and you doubt me?"

The freed dwarf closed her eyes in pain. "That's not Hertha." Then to Aleks and the others she said, "I'm Hillevi."

"Pleased to meet you," said Henrik, holding out a hand in greeting. "We've been trying to reach out in peace for some time, but were unable to do so because of the dragon's influence on the Ravagers."

As Hillevi reached out to take it, Saskia said frostily, freezing the dwarf in place, "The pleasure is not returned. Keep your hands to yourself and where I can see them. I don't trust you."

Hillevi dropped her hand. As the remaining confusion left her features, she nodded thoughtfully. "I wouldn't trust me either, but if what you're saying is true, that I was possessed by a dragon, I have to go warn my command."

"Not a chance," Saskia said. "If the Sixth Fox Throne War has taught me anything, it is that motive changes with circumstances. Right now you're friendly because we have you and your friend at our mercy; but back in your fold and surrounded by others of your ilk, you'll betray us."

"I wouldn't," Hillevi implored, with big brown eyes. She looked to Henrik for aid.

"You'll understand if we don't take your word for it," said Aleks, backing Saskia up, and earning himself a nod of approval from her. "You were, after all, just recently possessed."

Sighing, Henrik dropped his hand and sheathed his sword. "Another time then to make your official acquaintance," he said, apologetically. "If you'd be so kind as to turn around and place your hands behind your back, I'll tie you up."

"I don't have any more shoelaces to tie her up with," warned Aleks.

"Get Princess Zaria's," said Henrik. "I'll watch Hillevi. She won't make any hasty decisions."

Saskia snorted. With her foot she kicked away the spear. "You're too trusting Stag Lord."

Aleks carefully undid Zaria's laces so as not to jostle her awake. Taking them in hand, he went back to the Ravager where she reluctantly turned and presented to him her wrists. Everyone knew from elves to giants, dwarves to dragons, and everybody in between, that tying up an enemy's hands was the safest way to prevent a magical attack. Nobody liked it, of course, but everyone understood why it had to be done.

As he tied her up, securing the knot, she begged, "Please, I have to warn my sisters. I have to tell the king. I have to free Hertha."

"Out of the question," said Saskia, shaking her head. "Your command, by choice or not, is in cahoots with a dragon."

"Not to mention Brunhild admitted to taking orders from the traitor, Prince Floki. She is therefore compromised."

"I don't believe it," gasped Hillevi. "Not Lieutenant Brunhild. She's the best of us."

"Believe it," said Aleks, spinning her back around.

"But surely, we can free Hertha?" the dwarf woman pleaded.

"I'm afraid not," said Aleks. "Princess Zaria warned us that knocking her out —"

"Or killing her —" inserted Saskia.

Aleks ignored that. "— would free Fritjof to possess another. We can't risk that."

"Then what will you do with us, runt?" demanded Hertha, struggling against her bonds like a cat dead-set against getting wet.

"I suppose we'll take you back to the Autumn Court," he said, looking at his friends for better ideas.

"And toss you in the oubliette," confirmed Saskia. "You won't do any harm there."

Aleks shuddered at the thought, remembering the cramped hole. "Is that really necessary?"

"She's possessed by Fritjof," Saskia said, as if that alone made her point. He supposed it did.

"I don't like it," he admitted.

"You don't have to like it," countered Saskia.

He supposed he didn't. "As soon as we take care of Fritjof, we free her. Hillevi can be put in a prison cell. When I hear back from King Flein, we'll take the next steps."

"Of course," she said brightly, happy that he was being so reasonable. "Now let's secure our sorceress and get her back to the palace."

"That reminds me. How did she and these dwarves come to be here?" asked Henrik.

Aleks reached in his pocket for a coin and brushed against something squishy. He pulled it out to reveal an earplug. Fishing for the other he presented them to Saskia. "Put these in Hertha's ears."

She took them and planted a foot on the wiggling dwarf. Hertha tried to buck Saskia off her, but didn't have the leverage. With quick efficiency, Saskia stuffed the dwarf's ears with the earplugs and backed away. Hertha growled and flopped around on the floor, gnashing her teeth.

"That'll drown out some of our conversation," said Aleks. "Do you still have your earplugs, Henrik?"

He patted his pockets and nodded, pulling them out. He approached Hillevi, and she reared back in alarm. The Stag Lord hesitated.

Softly, he said, "I know it's unpleasant, but it's for your safety as much as it is for ours."

She eyed Saskia and Aleks before relenting, and allowed Henrik to plug her ears. "Happy?" she demanded, speaking louder than before.

"It'll have to do," Aleks said. He beckoned Saskia and Henrik closer, reaching into his pocket with his other hand. He felt around for coins, and brushed only one. Perturbed, he felt in his other pocket and found two more. He cursed.

"What's wrong?" Saskia asked, touching his elbow.

"I had more of them, but they must have fallen out during the fight. We'll have to collect them if we can find them."

"Find what?" asked Henrik.

Aleks opened his fist, revealing the three coins, careful to block them from view of the dwarves. He whispered, "I wished on one of these."

Saskia's eyebrows flew up to her hairline. "From the Lost Well?"

He nodded and stuffed the coins in his pocket. "There's a door behind me that opens at dusk. If I'm inside, it stays open until dawn."

The winter fairy quivered in excitement, but managed to maintain her composure. She didn't even try to look down the hallway. Her growing grin was full of fangs. "Has it granted every wish you've made on a coin?" she asked. "That's incredible. I've never heard of the well doing that."

Aleks shrugged. "It's a perk of being bonded to it, I guess. Were other kings and queens capable of unusual feats after becoming the monarch?"

"Now that you mention it, the Spring King, before he was king, was considered so weak his family almost excommunicated him as a changeling, even though they didn't have three kits. After claiming the throne he did astonishing magic, even types not typically in his court's purview. Everyone thought these hidden magical talents were why the well had chosen him."

"Doubtful," said Aleks. "He must have been making wishes."

"I know this war," said Henrik. "Wasn't this the one where your court aligned with Summer and attacked an engagement party between Autumn and Spring nobles? My great-great-great-grandfather Hagbard was there. He said Summer had blatantly ignored the laws on changelings."

Saskia nodded. "Winter knew that, but we aligned anyway. Our court followed the laws, but allowed ennobled powerful commoners into their ranks to swell their numbers. My family just missed the mark. My grandmother wasn't powerful enough for Carita's grandfather."

"That'll change," said Aleks, sensing the underlying bitterness. "Your family's rank will rise."

"All new nobles are sworn to support Carita's line and that of the Summer ruling line."

Aleks' eyes flashed. "Yours won't be. Nor anyone else I choose to elevate. This is not the sixth war."

"It's a good thing it isn't, too," Saskia whispered. "It was a dark time of fear and chaos for our realm. Sides switched constantly from one breath to the next. Nobody knew which alliance was being honored. Backdoor deals were made and broken with gusto as the courts positioned themselves for the throne."

"Who won?" asked Aleks.

"Summer, although Winter held the throne for a brief time after killing the Spring King. He lost his support, though, and quickly ceded the throne to Summer in a bid for mercy. The new Summer King rescinded the laws on changelings, obviously because they had broken it so egregiously. He also had many nieces and nephews. He should have known that his policies endangered them. They were all slain at his funeral."

"I guess the Lost Well doesn't make you smarter, just stronger," joked Aleks weakly, swallowing his appall. It felt like swallowing a rock. He cleared his throat. "Let's get these dwarves back to the Autumn Court."

Chapter Nine: Summer Court

Aleks and Henrik emerged into Niffleheim, following Saskia and the two dwarves, whom she guided in front of her. Straightening and shifting their precious load, they both grunted. Propped between them, Zaria hung like deadweight. She was once again unconscious and cool to the touch. Aleks worried about her, and he could tell Henrik did too.

"You weren't this bad," Aleks said quietly, surrendering Zaria to the Stag Lord.

Henrik hefted her into his arms, frowning down at her slack face. "No, but I don't have nearly as much magic as she does. These chains are designed to strip us of all magic – to keep us from accessing it."

Aleks looked at the possessed dwarf, remembering how Zaria helped him during the fight. Pitching his voice lower, he said, "It's pretty amazing she was able to cast anything then."

"She's pretty amazing," Henrik agreed.

Clearing his throat, Aleks ignored the inscrutable emotion on Henrik's face and called out to Saskia. "We're ready to keep moving."

Their little group hadn't time to take a step before Christoffer and Geirr appeared. Flying through the grasses, they crested the hill at a run with a quartet of foxes at their ankles. Surprising Aleks further, Zorka loped up the hill just behind them; her face set in a fierce mask, her rainbow hair secured in a single braid down her back.

When the two groups saw each other the boys' eyes widened. Whatever their intent had been, it shifted immediately upon seeing Zaria. With a cry of excitement, Christoffer surged forward, putting on speed Aleks hadn't seen since wolverines chased him down in Trolgar.

"How did you get her?" Geirr called out, relief flooding him as he raced over.

In seconds, Christoffer pulled her from Henrik's arms, propping her up on her feet. She moaned in response, her eyes flickering open, and he gave her a squeeze. "Hey Zaria," he murmured, looking her over to see if she was all right. "Does anything hurt? You're safe. We got you. You're safe."

"How is she?" Geirr asked, concern darkening his brow. He gently jostled Henrik out of the way and tucked himself under Zaria's arm, lending his strength.

Christoffer glanced at the two prisoners. "Did you rescue her from these dwarves?"

"We did," Aleks confirmed. "What are you all doing here?"

"We came to find you and to warn you about developments here," Zorka said. "Sivert recalled all his soldiers from the plains and diverted them to Summer Court."

Saskia jerked upright. She barked at the foxes to guard the dwarves. "Why did he do that? He was supposed to be looking for Zaria."

"One guess who," Geirr said darkly, then added, "You're father, Grimkell, is angling for the throne."

Christoffer's mouth skewed in distaste. "He apparently schemed an attack on Autumn within seconds of leaving the throne room. He planned it perfectly. Somehow he knew you weren't at court and tried a coup with his new alliance."

Angry, Aleks snarled, showing his fangs. "I knew I shouldn't have let him go free. Where is he now?"

"He's shielded by the Sommer Skyttergraven where he retreated," Geirr said.

"Then we'll have to retrieve him and put a stop to this. We'll never be able to go after Fritjof, if we keep fighting each other."

"Your sister has taken several Autumn foxes with her to do just that," Zorka said with a toothy grin. "She's sworn to do something to him that I don't think is anatomically possible. It was quite colorful. I like her better for it. Didn't know she had it in her."

Aleks chuckled mirthlessly. "Grimkell tends to bring out the uglier emotions in his progeny. He's about to see mine up close and personal."

The group quickly made their way to the grand building in the center of the Autumn Court. The foxes and Saskia veered off with the dwarves in tow to deposit them in a prison cell. Filip, who'd been left behind to coordinate any messages that needed to be relayed between parties, caught sight of Zaria and quit his agitated pacing to intercept them.

Running to her, he scooped her up in his arms and buried his face in her neck. His eyes were suspiciously wet, which created an uncomfortable lump in Aleks' throat. He looked away and stuffed his hands in his pockets. It was good to have her back. She glued them together, and they were all a little protective of her.

"We need to secure her somewhere safe and get to Summer Court," he said.

"I don't trust her with anyone but us," Filip said, clearing his throat.

"You can stay with her," Aleks offered. "But I can't stay. I have to go find my sister and Sivert. Then I have to deal with Grimkell's insurrection."

"I want to stay as well," said Christoffer.

"Then you should stay as well," said Aleks before focusing on the others. "I need to change into my armor before we leave."

Zorka plucked Zaria up in her arms, ignoring Filip's protests, and carried the princess to the wing set aside for palace guests. The blond teen trailed on her heels, following the troll to the top of the landing — Christoffer too, and they all disappeared.

Geirr followed Aleks to his rooms, where he leaned against the door frame and watched as Aleks pulled his armor out of the wardrobe and donned it. Seeing him struggle, Geirr came over and jerked the straps tight, clapping him on the back when he was through. Yawning, he flung himself into an armchair.

"Oh man, I'm tired," he said. "Nobody slept after you disappeared in a flash of red."

"I'd have been back sooner," Aleks said by way of apology.

Geirr waved that off. "Better that you found Zaria. Filip was going nuts, and he was making me crazy, too. I can't wait for this to be over."

"You and me both," admitted Aleks.

After a minute, Geirr said, "We've got to plan something fun for your birthday."

"My plans have changed," said Aleks, frowning at his laceless shoes.

"You'll always be king, now," said Geirr. "It'll never be over for you."

"I know," he said glumly, kicking off his shoes and looking for a pair of boots. "I wanted to go to university and study business."

"Who says you can't?" asked Geirr.

"How could I rule from afar?" countered Aleks, locating a pair of boots and stuffing his feet inside.

Geirr made a noncommittal sound before changing the topic. "I don't have to call you His Majesty or anything, do I? I mean once you are crowned."

"Don't you dare," Aleks said. He went to the side table and poured himself a glass of water. "Besides, what would Oskar's cousin think about that?"

"What?" Geirr asked, confused.

"'His Majesty is my cousin,'" Aleks quoted, affecting his speech to sound like the giant ruler's.

"Oh, you mean the giants. Heh. Good one." His levity leaving him, he sighed. "I'm anxious about the investigation results. I don't want to lose my pilot's license."

"You won't," Aleks assured him.

"If only you were investigating me," he said. "You, at least, know a dragon caused the crash and not me."

"Svein commended you on your quick reflexes. That has to count in your favor."

"I suppose," he agreed.

Aleks chugged the glass, backhanding his mouth. He set it down as a thought occurred to him, "Geirr, what if the wind blast from the dragon was recorded on the airfield? If it was, wouldn't that clear you?"

"It just might," said Geirr, his whole face brightening. "Yes, yes, I think it just might."

"Good," said Aleks. "Then it has to happen. If it doesn't, I'll make a wish for it."

"Wish?" asked Geirr, and Aleks explained to him the magic from the coins in the well, quietly and under his breath to keep anyone from overhearing. He didn't know where all the secret passages were and didn't want to risk it being widely known.

Afterwards, they sat in silence for a while, before Geirr broke it again, saying, "Hey Aleks, I don't know what help I can be, but if you need anything, ever, you'll let me know, right? I'll get cleared to fly again and charter fairies around Norway for you. Whenever you want. Best friend discount even."

Aleks laughed lightly. "Thanks Geirr, you're a true pal. If I ever need anything, I'll call you, first."

They returned to the grand entrance and met with Saskia and Zorka. The four checked their weapons for imperfections and secured them before departing. Extra arrows were retrieved from an armory for Aleks, which he placed in his wrist quiver. He thanked the young fox who brought them to him and put him in charge of seeing to his friends' needs, which turned out to be a big promotion by the huge grin and eagerness to which the fox took to his new role in the palace.

In the midday sun, rainbows glittered everywhere, dazzling the eyes. Aleks shielded his with a hand until his own sight adjusted. The way to Summer Court was tedious, picked over uneven earth, and long, as they circled the inland sea. They couldn't go through the plains because Zorka was too big to fit inside the tunnel, and without the creeper to wheel her along, Aleks and the others wouldn't be able to pull her through.

While Aleks and his friends climbed over boulders that bordered the woods around the courts, Zorka merely stepped over them as if they were stones. A pillar of smoke guided them to the crystal city, the seat of the Summer Court. As they neared, sounds of fighting disrupted the scene.

Something exploded against the tall crystal wall surrounding the city. It sent chunks of crystal flying. Another explosion ricocheted against the wall, breaking off more crystal shards. Hearing screams, Aleks picked up his pace. He just hoped they weren't too late.

Saskia came from behind, tackling him to the ground just as a flaming arrow thudded into the grass. In seconds, the flame scorched the area around it and died. She hauled him upright and thrust him hard against the wall beside Geirr, shielding him from their attackers.

Zorka didn't bother to shield herself from the arrows; her tough skin made her nearly invulnerable to this kind of attack. She grunted in displeasure, though, when one arrow caught her clothes on fire. She smothered it with a hand, glaring down at the charred remains of her shiny vest.

Saskia hissed to grab Aleks' attention. She gripped his shirt tighter, and snarled, "Red, don't you ever run toward a battle like that again. You were exposed. Had that arrow actually been aimed at you, you could have been killed. They're not regular arrows like yours, these are bespelled."

"Sorry," he said quickly, staring into her angry eyes. He feared more for his life in that moment than he had ever before. "I wasn't thinking."

"No, you weren't," she agreed mildly.

Zorka raised a hand over her eyes to ward off the reflective glare. Squinting, she spotted a fairy on top of the wall and pointed. Taking one large fist, she slammed it hard against the crystal. The resulting boom reverberated up the wall, where losing his footing, the fairy fell backwards and out of sight.

"Ouch," Geirr muttered, but his tone was appreciative. "You're strong."

"There'll be more where he came from," the troll warned. She gave Geirr an affectionate squeeze, nearly buckling him. "We better get moving."

"We need to find my father," Saskia said. "He's at the heart of this mess."

"He's just doing what he'd promised to do," Aleks reminded her. "Fight my enemies. It's my father who decided to declare himself as one."

"Summer's too for joining him," added Geirr. "Didn't they get the message you were king?"

"That's unclear right now," said Aleks. "If they didn't, then this is a travesty. If they did…"

He left the rest of his words unsaid. If Summer did know he was their king, then the infighting might turn into the next Fox Throne War, a war he might not survive. Saskia squeezed his hand, whether to reassure him or herself, he did not know.

"The Lost Well has been found, Aleks," she said. "War was inevitable as soon as that became common knowledge. It's not your fault."

"I never thought it was," he replied. "The well is the source for all of Niffleheim's problems. It instills such greed and covetousness."

"It can be a source for good," she reminded. "You found Zaria with the well."

"So many succumb to its siren call of unlimited power," he murmured.

"But not you," she said staunchly. "That's why you're going to be the greatest king Niffleheim has ever seen. You will make us better."

The earth shook beneath their feet as they crouch-ran along the wall, seeking the main gates into the Summer Court. They didn't need the entrance, however, as a large section of the wall had collapsed under some previous attack upon it. Making their way over the rubble and pieces of ice, the quartet slipped inside, Zorka shielding them with her body.

As arrows rained down on them, Aleks nearly gagged. He couldn't see blood, but the smell of iron overwhelmed his nose. Covering his face, he picked his way past broken buildings. As he looked closer, he saw limbs sticking out of the grimy snowy wreckage at odd angles. Fey were buried under the debris. Were they allies or enemies?

Those fortunate enough to be unburied were working together with others to release their friends. Many had wounds from their encounters with debris, arrows, or frostbite. Some paused to stare at them. Aleks knew they didn't recognize him. He was fortunate that the well graced him with a magic cuff and not an ostentatious crown.

The fey all gawked at Zorka. If it had been weird to see a changeling in Niffleheim, it was weirder still to see a troll. He waved, hoping the wounded would get the help they needed. In response, some of them bared fangs and hissed, but others were not so quick to judge. When everything was sorted out, he'd send some fairies over to assist.

Saskia, knowing the way from her reconnoitering, led them to the Summer Court's center. Aleks, abashed, couldn't concentrate enough to draw on his natural navigational talent. Everywhere he looked, he saw chaos and despair. This was the kingdom the well had chosen him for – a kingdom filled with hate and suspicion. Snow and flame clashed, hissing and spitting in jets of steam all around.

He couldn't fathom the destruction of lives and livelihoods. So many wars... too many... and they didn't need one more. This had to stop. He had to find Grimkell and Sivert and stop them from dragging any more fey into this conflict. The bloodshed had to stop. They had a greater enemy to face than each other. If only he could make Grimkell understand.

Aleks spotted Sivert before he spotted Grimkell. The general stood, feet braced apart, in the center of a large square surrounded by monolithic crystal buildings. All around him a sea of battle fraught with wild energy surged with the ebb and flow of magical attacks, as fey lobbed ice and fire, without regard to where the magic would land, helping and harming both friend and foe. Only Sivert seemed unaffected.

Large booms blasted against one building drawing Aleks' attention. Screams erupted as a few fey fell off the roof to their doom. Another choking blast impacted nearby, sending him scrambling for purchase. Hot vaporous columns rose from collisions between the factions, obscuring the scene.

His gaze traveled upward, where his brown eyes met his father's stormy ones. Grimkell sneered down his hooked nose at Aleks. He shouted something, pointing his way. Zorka yanked Aleks behind her and grunted when a flurry of fiery arrows hit against her and fell around them. Saskia stamped one flame out with her boot. Icicles formed in her hands, but she was too far away to fling them at the fairy on the roof.

Sivert glanced over his shoulder and grinned. "I've got him, Jelena, and Rex cornered. It won't be much longer by my calculations."

Aleks shot Saskia a questioning look. She explained, "Jelena and Rex are the current rulers of the Summer Court."

"I don't see them," Aleks said, searching the roofline.

"They're inside," grunted Sivert. "Sitting safely in their throne room... for now."

"Are you sure there aren't any escape tunnels?" asked Aleks. "The Autumn Court is rife with them. If Jelena and Rex thought Grimkell might lose, would they run?"

"I've seen the tunnels at Autumn Court myself," Saskia said.

"They're extensive and run throughout the court, but especially between the throne room and the family home," Aleks revealed.

Sivert's eyes widened and he cursed a blue streak; he had clearly neglected to plan for something. Aleks' eyebrows rose to his hairline. It seemed that his power wasn't the only one on the fritz if the greatest strategizer in Niffleheim had forgotten that fox tunnels ran rampant. Fritjof's influence was gaining a deeper foothold.

Pointing with one of his daggers, the general ordered a team on his left to charge the doors and get inside no matter the cost. They were to capture the Summer rulers and bring them to him. When they left, he directed the team on his right to launch another flurry of cannonballs.

Grimkell shouted to his troops and braced himself as an icy cannonball lobbed through the air and landed with deadly accuracy against the side of the building. The foundations shook, but no fairies fell from their positions. They readied their counterattack.

Sivert's stoic expression never flinched as the rain of fire hissed and spit against a sudden pillar of ice which erupted from the earth in front of him. He gave a nod of appreciation to the female fairy who'd put up the block. She smiled and the ice sunk back into the ground.

"Troll, can you climb that building?" asked Sivert, calmly.

Zorka rubbed her hands in glee. "You only had to ask." She turned to Aleks with a conspiratorial grin. "Forget setting off bombs with Falkor; Kanutte is going to be insanely jealous when I tell her about this. She'll turn a perfect shade of green."

Sivert rubbed a blade against his cheek. "I didn't understand half of that, but I need you to get up there and get that puffed up idiot wearing that mangy fur cloak."

"Yes sir," she saluted and took off at a lumbering sprint.

Watching her go, Sivert sneered, "Grimkell couldn't hold his own court, what makes him think he can go against you, son? You wrested the Autumn court away from his sister and laid claim to the others. He can't be thinking clearly."

Aleks grunted in assent. Zorka reached the building and spat on her hands, looking for a good place to grab hold. It would be tough to find when the building is polished crystal. Grimkell ignored her at first, focusing intently on Aleks and the Winter general.

Saskia shoved Aleks and Geirr forward, so they were behind Sivert and the protection of the ice shields. She looked to her father, and he ordered her to find that wretched redheaded girl and help her team. Aleks assumed he meant Nori. He looked for his sister, hoping to spy her through the dust clouds.

"Son, you and your friend need to stay down and stay out of my way. Gisele, keep them guarded."

"But sir," she protested. "What about you?"

"I gave my order," he said.

"Yes sir," she answered obediently, while shooting Aleks and Geirr a venomous glare.

Aleks didn't expect her to follow orders, but didn't have time to worry about it. He shifted his gaze from following Saskia's retreat to focus on Zorka. She'd decided against climbing from the bottom. With a horrendous battle cry, she leapt.

Boom.

Her landing rattled the building, causing Grimkell and his fairies to stumble. Aleks suppressed a cheer, but he couldn't suppress the gasp that came unbidden when Zorka began to slip. She scrabbled for purchase, her weight pulling her down faster and faster. She didn't think. Screwing up her legs, she pushed and leapt upward with all her might.

"I can't watch this," moaned Geirr, hands on his head. "She's going to fall."

Boom.

"She didn't," breathed Aleks, relieved.

Clinging to the edge of the building, still slipping downward, Zorka got her feet under her. She bent at the knees and pushed, – which to Aleks' eyes appeared to tilt the building – launching herself higher still.

Boom.

His father and the fairies with him, couldn't keep their balance. He barked orders, but nobody could carry them out, unable to stand. They could barely hold on. She leapt again.

Boom.

Like a baby Godzilla, Zorka scaled the building. Halfway up, she readied herself again, only for an ice cannonball to smash into the building on her left. She reared away from the shrapnel, turning her head aside. Then slipped and nearly fell.

Aleks spun on his heel, snarling at the trio throwing them. "If you can't aim then don't throw any."

"Agreed," barked Sivert. "The troll is with us."

Geirr cheered, drawing Aleks' attention back to the rainbow-haired troll. She yelled like a pirate, swinging her heavy body up like a gymnast on bars. With a daring, breath-defying grab that stretched out her whole body, Zorka sunk her hand into the new handhold provided by the three idiots.

Higher now, she hadn't much farther to go. Grimkell seemed to realize this and shoved his fey closer to her, willing to sacrifice them to gain a small advantage. When Zorka jumped again, those too close toppled over the edge. One fey with short-cropped brown hair managed to cushion his fall with a bed of springy grass erupting from the ground.

Aleks glared at his father, not that his parent noticed. Grimkell whipped up a fierce wind, sending it whiplashing down on the troll. Her hair blew back from her head in a straight line, her clothes swirled in every direction, and her eyes streamed water, even half-closed against the force of the air hitting her face. She roared into the wind, baring every tooth in her mouth, including the gap where one tooth was missing.

Aleks spied the fey with the bow and arrow first, taking aim at Zorka's face. Barely thinking he drew his own bow and winged an arrow at the creature. He hit the fey in the leg, dropping him. He drew another arrow and notched it, aiming at his father.

Releasing a pent up breath, he concentrated and let it fly. The arrow whizzed through the hurricane winds, and blew off course. He growled in frustration and slung his bow across his back. His father's power wouldn't be countered by mere arrows.

He would need his uncle's slashing power, which wasn't affected by the winds Grimkell drew upon. Too bad he wasn't here to put a tear in his father's sails. Not that he'd want Ytorm at his side; the man was an untrustworthy ninny who belonged in his prison cell.

Aleks watched as Zorka made one last outrageous jump and reached the top of the flat-roofed crystal building. Even clinging with one hand to the edge of the roof, she seemed secure. Grimkell glowered and put more effort into his attack. She didn't care and with almost casual ease swung herself over the side of the building and clambered to her feet.

"It takes more than a stiff breeze to do me in," she said cheerfully, and with one punch, clocked Grimkell so hard he fell down in an ignominious heap.

Let that be a lesson to all. As cool as having wind power may be, it can't block a fist to the face. Also, don't piss off a troll.

Chapter Ten: The Seventh Fox Throne War

Nori and Saskia appeared on the roof. The sight of both caused Sivert to roar with pleasure. All around them fey cheered. Victory was theirs.

The fey that had sided with Grimkell dropped their weapons and sunk to their knees, instantly contrite and unwilling to shed blood for a defeated general. Sivert's soldiers rounded them up, binding several in ropes, securing their hands behind their backs. Aleks wasn't sure what he should do with them. Leniency might be best, but it also might be the dumbest thing he could do.

Throughout the surrender, Aleks wondered where his brother was. Lukas' absence left a taste of foreboding on his tongue. He caught Nori's gaze and saw the same foreboding etched there. There wasn't time to dwell on it though, because more pressing matters needed his attention.

Summer Court writhed in the midst of sudden change. With its rulers Jelena and Rex on the lam, its ally Grimkell and many of its best fighters captured, nobody knew where to look for leadership. Aleks' presence was unwelcome and mistrusted, causing more strife within the court. It took all of Sivert's soldiers to round up the malcontents and rustle them into something orderly.

Aleks stood before them on a balcony just outside the throne room in their Sommer Skyttergraven, looking down at a sea of wary and mutinous faces. He found himself at a loss for words. How could he address their fears, calm them, and rouse them from the mire that Fritjof was casting like a fishing net over Niffleheim? Why would they rally to him? They didn't even know him.

Geirr peered out from the shadows inside the court room to offer support. "It's a good thing you don't have a fear of public speaking."

"Might be a good time to develop one," Aleks muttered. "Does this even have the smallest change of working?"

"Chin up," Nori coached from just behind him. "You have to project confidence."

"The troll who is loudest is heard the most," said Zorka, offering her thoughts on the matter.

Saskia peered out from the other side of the throne doors. "Stop whining. Straighten up and let them know you're their king."

Aleks squared his shoulders and raised a hand. He cleared his throat. The mutterings ceased, as all strained to hear him.

"I know you're all wondering what's going to happen next. Your rulers have fled, Winter soldiers are all around you, and then there's me. I am sure many of you don't know what to make of me. You've probably never seen me before..." he paused, took a breath and continued, "I'm Aleks Mickelsen. I'm a changeling, and I am your king."

A loud outcry came from the throng. Nori whistled, bringing them back to themselves.

Aleks nodded his thanks. "I found the Lost Well and bonded with it. I know this comes as a great shock, so let it be clear to you all that I have no interest in a divided Niffleheim. We must unite as one, and we must hurry. Niffleheim doesn't have the luxury to sort itself out in its own sweet time. A dragon threatens the very fabric of your lives."

Another outcry rose, but a second sharp whistle from Nori silenced them.

"A dragon by the name of Fritjof has removed all memories of his name from your minds, but you'll remember him as the dragon who tunneled between Jerndor and Niffleheim, creating the Thief of Peace's Passage."

Gasps and yips filled the square, but instantly hushed as Nori made a move to bring her fingers to her mouth. No one wanted another piercing whistle.

"Liar!" shouted a brave soul in the crowd.

Aleks found the woman, her chin thrust forward, blonde hair and skin caked in grime from the skirmish between Summer and Winter. He gave her a pitying, kindly smile.

"Am I? Look around you. Is this not utter madness? Why are we fighting each other? Why fight the dwarves? For what purpose does it suit anyone? Why enslave brownies when they'd happily work and protect Niffleheim? Why are we divided against ourselves? Why turn some fey into changelings? Why fight brother against sister? Father against son? Mother against daughter?

"Why look for true substance at the bottom of a well? True power isn't found in material belongings, but you're all blind to that because a dragon rules over you. A sinister, creeping malfeasance like him would rot Niffleheim from the inside out. Don't stand for it. Fight."

"Changeling," the woman spat, her face screwing up like it had tasted something bitter.

"King," retorted Aleks, spinning on his heel and walking back toward the open doors. He ignored the crowd's increasing volume, as they talked and shouted over his passionate words.

"Good on you," said Zorka, moving aside for him.

Geirr gazed at him with eyes wide in awe. "You're like King freaking Arthur."

"No, just King Aleks," he quipped back, slapping his friend on the shoulder. "No knights at the round table here."

"Funny," said Geirr, composing himself. "Because I think Filip would be the first to apply."

Aleks snorted. "Does that make Zaria my Merlin?"

Geirr elbowed him in the ribs. "It makes Saskia your Guinevere."

Aleks shoved him away. "*Lancelot!*"

Geirr laughed, swiveling out of reach as Aleks gave chase. Saskia laughed too, shutting the doors on the crowds below. The sound of her laughter caused Aleks to misstep. He took two more to cover the fact, feeling his ears warm.

"You know who Guinevere was?" he asked.

She shook her head, smiling. "Not a clue, but I like watching you squirm."

"I know," said Nori, conspiratorially.

"Ah, there's Morgan Le Fay," Aleks groused, causing Geirr to snicker and Nori to glower.

Inside the throne room, Sivert leaned against a vine-covered wall, picking at his nails with his knife. "Some speech, son," he rasped. "You'll galvanize them to act, no doubt, but will you like the results?"

The crowd outside erupted into a frenzy, drawing everyone's attention. Aleks raced to balcony doors, and stared mutely down on the crowd, horror filling him, as they tore each other apart. Soldiers in the crowd struggled to break up the rioting mob. He wanted to fling open the doors and rage at them all for their stupid fighting, but Zorka was there, blocking him.

"Let me out," he demanded.

"It's not safe, baby brother," said Nori.

"They're playing into Fritjof's hands," he growled.

"So be it," said Zorka. "Better than you playing into theirs, and ultimately his. They're not in the right mind to listen. You'll have to wait until later and address whoever is left."

With a heavy heart, Aleks gazed around the throne room, as if seeing it for the first time. Covered in curtains of green vines, flowers, and sun motifs, the Sommer Skyttergraven gave off a much friendlier vibe than the one in Autumn's court. It smelled like paradise, cleansing Aleks' nose of the blood and gore from outside.

"Sivert, sir," a soldier said, bursting through the throne room's entrance. "Come quick."

Sivert flipped the knife over, catching it by the hilt. "What is it, Klas?"

"We got a new lead on Jelena and Rex." Klas cut his gaze to Aleks, hesitating.

Aleks knew why. Even though he, too, worried that Sivert's soldiers hadn't yet found Jelena or Rex, he had forbidden interrogation of the Summer fey left in the palace. He didn't want to turn its workers on the defensive, fearing for their lives and their families. He wanted to start his reign with trust by ruling out fear.

Upon gaining access, he'd promised a full pardon for attacking their rightful king if they laid down their arms. All of them did, staring at him in awe, causing him to wonder again what he did to make them look at him that way. Were leniency and mercy so uncommon as to seem miraculous?

"New lead?" asked Aleks. Klas, a stern Winter fairy, clamped his mouth shut. He cocked an eyebrow. "What's the lead? How did you get it?"

"Grimkell," he bit out.

The other eyebrow flew up. "My father?"

Grimkell was bound tightly and locked securely in one of Summer's dungeon cells so that he wouldn't even be able to scratch an itch on his great big nose. Sivert pressed that he be slain, saying, "The fox and the dog do not play together." Aleks, however, couldn't make that order and spared him, no matter how convincingly and persuasively the general spoke.

No, Grimkell's fate would be decided at a special Firething called for in the morning. That had been Nori's idea. There, in front of the other courts, his deeds would be made known, and they would judge him by his actions. Calling the Firething also gave Aleks the opportunity to meet everyone and formally declare his rule. Three palace servants, each accompanied by a guard, had rushed out with the messages.

He turned to his sister, observing her drawn face. "Maybe you should verify what he says."

Nori's ability to know the truth meant that no lie would deceive her. Grimkell had every reason to lie, and none to tell the truth. Having Nori listen to Grimkell and weigh his words would put them on a better footing than simply going by Klas' perception of his interrogation skills.

"As you wish," she said, and beckoned to Klas to show her the way.

"I'll join her," said Zorka, cracking her knuckles. "My fists might come in handy."

Later that night, Nori met Aleks in the Summer throne room. Standing behind his shoulder, she stared at the bleak square below. The riot had left its mark. The buildings were crumpled heaps, utterly unsalvageable. The soldiers, with Zorka's help, had managed to keep them from reaching the Sommer Skyttergraven, but it had left the rest of the city defenseless. It was clear Fritjof had won another round.

He met her gaze in the crystal window. Only her brown eyes showed emotion. They glittered with hatred. He wondered if it was directed at him; after all, from her point of view, he had caused this. His very presence in Niffleheim had caused this senseless war.

"I'm sorry," he said to her. "I didn't want this to happen. Any of it."

"That's why I wanted the throne," she said harshly, her voice raw. She turned away from him. "A changeling has never been crowned. It was too much for them to accept."

He snapped, "Then why tell the Autumn Court I'm king?"

Fury thinned her face, but instead of barking at him, she swallowed it and walked away. "I had no choice."

"Of course you had a choice," said Aleks. "You could have claimed it for yourself."

"No, I couldn't," she conceded wearily, sliding down against a vine-covered wall. "I couldn't fight the truth anymore. You're king."

Aleks groaned, tugging his hair by its roots "This is so messed up. Why me? Who says? You? What made you think so? How can a baby be seen as a king?"

Her red hair, dulled under layers of dirt, bristled. "I have always been able to see the truth."

"Right," agreed Aleks, steeped in bitterness. "You're the best lie detector there is —"

She sighed, "I am more than that. I see things plainly. The moment I held you, I knew you were destined to be king. I felt it."

"Felt it? That's a bunch of hogwash. Felt it, how? Explain," he demanded.

She made a vague gesture with her hands. "How does Zaria perform magic? How do you sense direction? It's the same with me. I just do it. I don't even have to think about it. When I held you in my arms, I knew in my gut that one day you'd eclipse mother, Lukas, and me in power, in stature... that you'd eclipse even father."

"And that feeling translated into the fact that I'd be king of Niffleheim, and not simply ruler of the Autumn Court," Aleks said dryly, not bothering to put his words into question form. He knew the answer before she spoke.

Nori's lips twisted wryly. She tucked a lock of her hair behind her ears. "Yes. As soon as I put words to it I sensed the truth of it even more. Grimkell thought that by leaving you a changeling, he could at once fulfill his promise to mother and escape your fate...

and his — by association. After all, you'd never come back to Niffleheim. Why would you? How could you? There'd be no reason for you to return."

"I wouldn't have, if it had meant this," said Aleks, nodding toward the city and the wounded foxes limping around the darkened streets. "But you asked me to come... you needed me."

"So I did," Nori said, hanging her head. "That's my fault. I thought it'd be safe. I thought I could use you and your friends to stop Fritjof, claim the Lost Well for myself, and be crowned queen. I'd protect my people, and your destiny would have been averted for a while longer. You'd have to wait until I died before the throne could be yours, but I was wrong.

"I could not will our fates to be switched. Father could not prevent it, either. Even with you fighting against your fate, there was no way to stem the tide of change. Whether you were destined by the happenstance of fortune, by a deliberate twist of fate itself, or God, you were meant to be king. I saw it clearly when you reentered the throne room after completing your trials.

"It was over, this vain struggle for the throne. Fighting your destiny was useless. It was never meant to be me. I would never be queen. It was always meant to be you. So I helped you... but I would not have your win be pyrrhic. A king must have a kingdom to rule. Our people needed a leader, not more bloodshed."

Aleks kicked at the window and crossed his arms. "Unfortunately they got both. I should never have followed you back here. Not even with the threat of a dragon looming over this place."

She glanced sideways at him, judging his words; then got up, went to the balcony doors, and thrust them open. He followed her outside. Nori let out a weary sigh and leaned against the railing. "That's the thing about destiny. We could have killed you as a babe, and somehow you'd still be here today as king of Niffleheim."

Joining her, Aleks said dryly, "Thank you for not making me one of the undead. At least there's that small silver lining to all of this."

She laughed humorlessly. "At least there's that, baby brother."

He exhaled and butted shoulders with her. "Thanks for trying to avert my fate. You're not the worst sister in the world. If it could've been anyone else to be ruler of the fey, I'd have picked you."

She flashed him a sad half-smile. "Not Saskia?"

He smiled and shrugged. "She's a little bloodthirsty."

Nori laughed. "So am I, but I see what you mean. I helped crown you in the end because you're not the worst brother in the world. If we can keep this war from spreading and stop Fritjof, you might even have a chance to be one of Niffleheim's greatest rulers, and wouldn't that be something to see?"

"What about the vote tomorrow?" he asked, turning around and leaning back against the balustrade. "What do you think they'll do to Grimkell? What about me?"

Nori copied him, staring up at the silvery icy dome above, which kept Niffleheim from being visible to humans. "Don't worry about the Firething. They can't rail against your reign any more than we could, or any more than Summer could. They certainly can't undo it with a vote, or demand you show the location of the Lost Well to prove the validity of your claim."

"That's good to know," said Aleks. "I don't really want its location to be common knowledge. What will they say about the treaties and laws from the previous Fox Throne Wars?

"They can say there are laws. They can even say there are rules, but the fact of the matter is, that as king, you make the laws. You set the rules. A changeling king is not illegal, if you say it's not. If you have the alliances and the promises on your side, you can even undo the treaties from the Fox Throne Wars."

"There's a thought," said Aleks. He turned to her, holding out his hand. "I'll need a royal advisor. What do you say? Will you be my right-hand woman tomorrow?"

She looked touched. She grasped his hand firmly and smiled a genuine smile. "I'd be honored, my liege."

"That sounds so weird," Aleks said with an exaggerated shudder.

"Don't get used to it," Nori said lightly. "I'll only break it out for truly special occasions. You're still my little brother. I can't let you get too big a head after all. Saskia would never forgive me if I did."

As if she'd been summoned, Saskia floated into the room. "She's right. If you got to be so arrogant your head couldn't fit through a doorway, I'd probably have to 'break up' with you."

"I thought you didn't know anything about dating," said Aleks, perplexed.

Nori laughed. "I think Saskia keeps you in line better than I can."

"For as much as you two don't seem to like each other, you both like to gang up on me," Aleks grumbled. He raised an eyebrow at Saskia. "Who told you what a break-up is?"

"I'll never tell," she said with a mysterious twinkle.

Aleks pouted. "I'm going to murder Christoffer."

"Why do you expect it's him?" asked Geirr, who'd slipped into the room behind the Winter fairy.

"Are you saying it was you?" Aleks asked, surprised. "You really are Lancelot!"

Geirr put on an innocent expression. "Why would you suspect me? It's Christoffer who is in constant need of a wingman, not I. His pool of available guy friends is dwindling fast."

"Luckily, there's still you," Aleks deadpanned.

"I thought you were my friend," Geirr joked. "Being Christoffer's wingman is no fun. He steals all the ladies' attention."

Nori and Saskia rolled their eyes, amused. Saskia grabbed Aleks' arm and dragged him back inside. "Come on, dinner is about to be served."

Dinner with the rest of Summer was an interesting affair. Considering Aleks didn't have much to compare it to, having never dined with Autumn, he decided to reserve judgment. One of the more talented fairies came in and grew tables made of grass from the floor. They spiraled outward like a rhythmic gymnast's ribbons, encircling the room.

Over a feast of Aleks' favorite foods, which he assumed Geirr had told the kitchens, Summer fey ate alongside Winter and Autumn. It wasn't always easy, there'd been some tense moments in the beginning, but Aleks' words at the start of the feast had kept everyone on their best manners.

Geirr and Zorka sat in the crowd between Winter soldiers and Summer palace servants. They regaled the crowd with stories about their adventures thus far. Their rapt audience hung on every word. Many didn't know whether to believe the stories or to take them with a grain of salt. Metal flying machines crashing to earth by dragon's breath? It didn't seem real.

Nori and Saskia sat on either side of Aleks, with Sivert across from him. Nori had just finished explaining that Grimkell's story about knowing where Jelena and Rex were was truth wrapped in a lie. Something wasn't quite right, but she hadn't put her finger on what it was just yet.

Sivert cussed, slamming his knife point-down in the leafy table. "We can't have another Seventh Fox Throne War on our hands."

Saskia gripped his forearm. "It won't be. Aleks is uniting, not dividing us."

"What happened?" asked Aleks.

"Fritjof was wreaking havoc in Jerndor, but when Autumn attacked at the funeral of the Summer king, the resulting bloodshed and chaos drew his attention to us," Nori said, putting down her utensils. "He came from Jerndor, burrowing in the earth like a great big worm."

"Fight for the throne intermingled with the fight for survival," Sivert said, jerking his blade out of the clinging vegetation. "I was a young man then."

"Like Grimkell?" asked Aleks.

He nodded. "We're a couple of old farts now, but back then we both thought that the best way to end the madness was to work with Queen Helena and the other leaders to stop the dragons."

Aleks sat there remembering all he'd heard about the Dragomir Treaty. "Your agreement meant supplying the void for the Under Realm."

"It also lost us the well," reminded Nori.

He nodded thoughtfully. "Yes, but ultimately it was for the best."

Sivert pointed the knife at him. "Don't say that at the Firething tomorrow, son, or you'll be ripped apart."

Aleks pushed the weapon aside with his dinner knife. "Without the well in play, you've all ruled your own courts autonomously."

Saskia pulled Aleks back. "Fighting and power struggles still break out, Red. Well or no well."

Sivert snorted in contempt. "What you three don't seem to realize is that without the well in play, the fey have lost much of their power. There are fewer and fewer truly talented fey born."

Nori jerked in her seat. "My father has said that magic has bled out of Niffleheim. He said that his father and his grandfather wielded much stronger magic. I didn't believe him."

"Believe him," Sivert said brusquely. "We weren't always limited to a single talent and the ability to shapeshift. That is why the return of the Lost Well is so important. That is why more than anything else, everyone will suck up to you, son. For the chance to find the well, to get their hands on it, to control it, and ultimately, hopefully, to reinstate the glory of earlier times.

"You will have more support than you could ever imagine, and all of it will be false. One wrong move and there'll be a knife in your back faster than you can say kettupeli."

Chapter Eleven: The Firething

The plan for this morning was far from simple. Each had their role to play, like little cogs in a political machine. Nori left first, gathering the Autumn crown for his coronation, and a contingent of Autumn fey along the way. She would arrive early and use the extra pairs of eyes and ears to scout for danger, essentially looking for Jelena and Rex in the gathering crowd.

Saskia escorted Grimkell to his reckoning. She took extra pleasure from prodding him in the back, forcing him to stumble along ahead of them in an ungainly and undignified manner, his oversize fur-collar cloak dragging through the dirt. Aleks knew that galled his father more than anything else. It was a brilliant and ruthless move. He sort of loved her for it.

Geirr and Zorka took off with the hulking Winter twins Emrik and Eckart to collect Filip, Christoffer, and Henrik. Zorka would remain behind to guard Zaria while the others came to present a united front. They, too, would arrive before him. Henrik was the one most needed at the Firething because of his status as Stag Lord of the ellefolken, to represent to all a unity of forces, a showing of alliances. If Zaria could've been present, that would have been even better. Aleks hoped they'd recover the Drakeland sword soon in order to free her from the chains.

Last to leave the Summer court were Sivert and Aleks. Sivert would go with Aleks as far as he could, bringing his soldiers as protection, but eventually he'd have to break off and appear beside Carita, the Winter ruler, if only for a short time. Soon his true allegiance would be made known, and Carita would have to fall in line or risk fighting her general.

Alone, Aleks would make a grand entrance, sweeping through the pair of monoliths that guarded the inner sanctum of the Firething. A pair of brownies had answered his tentative call the night before. Having freed them, Aleks hadn't been sure any had stayed, but at least these two had. Eagerly they took up the task, sprucing his clothing, so that his appearance was at its very best and even though they protested, he granted them a boon in the form of a wish each.

One wished to speak to their family in Finland and one wished for more talent in cooking. Each wish was accompanied by a red flare as the coins were spent and disappeared. The first brownie received a small cosmetic hand mirror, which Aleks guessed would act similarly to the mirror still in Falkor's grasp in Trolgar albeit on a less grand scale. It would only work for this brownie to find its family. Thus two of his fey coins were spent and he was down to one. Aleks wouldn't be able to replenish until it was safe to travel in the plains on his own.

The brownies' work was perfection. The armor shone, freshly oiled and repaired. The helmet gleamed like freshly cast silver. His cuff, which kept him from slipping back to the well in his sleep, had been cleaned of dirt and grime. He'd been gifted a set of clothes from a Summer noble, whose son he'd spared the night before. His fine leather boots were scrubbed and polished. He cut a fine and dashing figure, and he knew Saskia would approve.

Before departing, there was one last thing the brownies had done for him. They had each given him a small blessing – for protection they had said. And whether or not the blessings were the work of prayer or magic, Aleks still felt them fall upon his shoulders like a soft mantle of silk. The very idea of them made him feel warm and cared for and these were things he very much needed going forward.

He approached the Firething with strong, confident strides that ate up the earth. Someone in the crowd noticed him, ally or enemy he didn't know or care, and the noise ceased. All that mattered to him was making it through this ordeal, preferably alive and in one piece.

He passed the quieting gathering, nodding to Nori and Sivert, as he entered the horseshoe-shaped arena, and waved jauntily to his friends despite the nerves stinging his insides like angry swarming fire ants. Nobles sat on the stone benches with their followers standing behind them on wooden stands. Foxes slinked here and there, through ankles and around seats, whispering in the ears of many fey. The judging had begun, and it wasn't for Grimkell. They were all sizing him up to see if he was worthy, to see if they could defeat him.

Aleks made his way to the crystal thrones, uncomfortably aware that Sivert and his soldiers were the furthest from him that they could get, guarding the entrance and not his back. He wondered what story the old general had shared with Carita to bring her and the rest of the Winter Court here. He scanned them looking for her, but not knowing what she looked like his eyes slid past that section without resting on anyone.

A few Summer Court fairies were positioned on his left, which he wasn't too keen on, because of the riot that had broken out over his rule just yesterday. He couldn't move them and wasn't sure he should, as it would cause more tensions to arise, and, truthfully, it was probably best to have the frenemy he knew versus the enemy he didn't.

Thankfully, Nori and the rest of the Autumn Court were situated on his right. He recognized faces in that sector and while he didn't know names for many of them, he would someday. He hoped their turnout would temper any attempts to overthrow him before he was even crowned.

His feet stopped before the glittering slabs and shafts that made up the Fox Throne. Spinning around, Aleks slung himself into the seat and splayed his elbows on the armrests. He gazed at the representatives before him and prayed for the wisdom to navigate through the dark and dangerous waters. He took a calming breath and let it out slowly.

"Let's call this Firething to order, shall we?" he said, looking over steepled fingers.

"You should be killed," snarled a red fox, slinking into the center.

It didn't surprise Aleks that the first objector came from his own house. The best thing to do would be to act like grass – tough, elastic, and resilient. He wouldn't break because of them.

"According to whom?" he asked. "Are you king, here?"

"It's the law," the red fox insisted.

"I concur," said a gray fox. "You're an abomination."

Aleks snorted. "So says the coward unwilling to show his face."

A shift of light and they shed their skins. He looked at his accusers and rolled his eyes. A pair of scrawny teens with ruddy cheeks glared at him with hatred sizzling in their eyes. He'd get nowhere arguing against them.

"My breath is wasted on the likes of you. Sit. Down." he commanded.

The redheaded Autumn teen looked affronted and puffed out his meager chest. Aleks sincerely hoped he, himself, didn't look like that to the observers on the field. How embarrassing that would be.

"Run along," he murmured, shooing the boy away like a naughty child, despite appearing to be of a similar age. He understood how ironic that was. "Take your little friend with you. I will commend you on crossing house lines at least. Niffleheim can't afford false friendships."

The crowd said nothing as the duo scampered back into the throng. Aleks had a feeling these boys had been sent to test the waters to see how he'd react. He hoped his firm dismissal of them counted in his favor.

"You claim you've found the Lost Well," an older woman said, leaning forward on her seat.

"Is there a question?" he asked, canting his head.

She smiled like a fox in a henhouse. "Only Niffleheim's rightful ruler could access the Lost Well. Tell me where it is, and I will gladly go to verify your claim."

"Not a chance," said Aleks, laughing at her. "I will never reveal its location. It's my protection against all backstabbers and outright murderers. If I die, I will take with me the well's location."

She fairly thrummed with angry energy, but another voice overshadowed hers. A male with pale yellow hair stood and made his way to the inner circle. "If you won't reveal the location, how will you prove your claim to it? This could be a hoax."

"I've seen it with my very own eyes," said Nori, standing up.

"In that case, you should be ruler, not he."

Nori looked down her nose at him and sniffed. "The well did not grant my wish. It did not bond with me."

"He's nothing but a changeling," he grunted. "You know the laws."

"I know that as king I can change them to whatever I want," Aleks drawled. "I could force each of you to stand on one foot for an hour every day and spend another scrubbing a troll's backside. Don't test me."

An older, graying, Spring man stood up. "The pup is right about the laws. You know how it's been since Queen Raisa and the First Fox Throne War."

"Whose side are you on, Larin? The boy didn't even try to align with us," snarled a young man, jerking the older man to his seat.

Nori sniffed and said disdainfully, "We tried to be equal in our approach, but if your court wasn't able to get the message, that is on you. We aligned with the strongest of houses."

"I made no such agreement," said a woman with long white hair braided to her waist. She made her way to the center, pushing the blustering fey out of the circle. Her large kohl-lined turquoise eyes saved her from looking like a colorless ice queen.

"Carita," Nori acknowledged civilly. "Are you saying you're not the strongest of houses? It's so good of you to finally admit to your inferiority."

Carita's eyes flared with cold, glacial fire. "Watch your tongue vixen, or you may just find it cut out from your pretty head."

"Now, now," said Aleks with forced levity. "If anyone gets that honor it's me. God knows sisters can be annoying."

"Really," huffed Nori, rolling her eyes, but her lips quirked in amusement. "You think brothers are any better?"

He grinned at her, then looked at Carita. "What can I do for you?"

"I want proof of your claim. Perform magic."

Aleks arched an eyebrow. "That's very vague, but as you wish."

He thought about it for a minute and felt himself shift. The glittering sparkles following his transformation faded. Several around the circle gasped. They knew that a changeling lost his ability to transform into a fox after a lengthy stay amongst humans (all assumed it was the exposure to iron.) This one trick should be enough to back his claim.

Looking at the Winter ruler, he asked with forced amiability, "Proof enough for you?"

"Hardly," she declared. "Any kit worth his tail can transform into a fox. Why care I if you can?"

He flicked his tail and licked a paw. "What would convince you?"

"What's your true gift?" she demanded.

"And have you try to use it against me?" he tutted. "It's not flashy, but it's how I found Henrik, Stag Lord of the ellefolken, and freed him from Koll's clutches. It's how I found and freed a dozen troll children from prison. It's how I found the Lost Well. Just like my sister, you'll find me hard to trick."

She sneered at Nori. "Her gift is weak, probably just like yours. Niffleheim doesn't need another weak ruler."

Aleks transformed and took a step away from the thrones before Nori could explode all over the pompous Winter fairy. He dared to circle her, and came to a standstill a few inches from her. He was pleased to note he was taller than this woman.

"My sister's power is greater than everyone's here, including mine," he stated quietly, earning a rash of whispers. "She alone out of everyone retained her memories after a dragon wiped his very name from everyone's mind. She warned you, and when nobody heeded her, she came to me."

"Worse and worse," murmured Carita. "Resorting to changelings for help? Friends with the Stag Lord? I also heard rumors about Queen Helena's daughter. Don't you remember what happened the last time outsiders *helped* us?"

The whisperings turned angry and heated. Aleks felt them prickle against his skin. He canvassed the crowd for Sivert. The general dipped his head at him in silent support. Aleks turned back to Carita.

"It looks to me like Niffleheim is still standing, thanks to outsiders."

"But we lost our well," she reminded him and everyone. "That was a great blow."

"You deserved worse," he told her. "It wasn't destroyed, merely hidden for all of your protection. I've heard about your Fox Throne Wars, all seven of them, and you're lucky you didn't kill yourselves off. By all rights the fey should be extinct."

"You know nothing," she swore at him, her turquoise eyes shooting daggers.

"*You* know nothing," he returned. "You have no power here."

"I am the reigning noble of the Winter Court; my vote is something you should court, pup," she hissed.

"I think your power base has shifted without your notice, and I think you'll find your vote is no longer required. If you have complaints about it, that is as my sister put it earlier, on you."

She gaped at him and scoured the crowd for Sivert. "You wouldn't dare," she muttered. "Your loyalty is to me."

"Aleks made a better offer," he said.

She looked to her soldiers in the crowd and none would meet her gaze. "All of you? Are you so feckless and stupid as to follow a changeling?"

Eckart, or was it Emrik, looked at his brother, then back to Carita. "Under you we would be fettered."

"The changeling offers us greater freedoms and opportunities."

"The old ways are over."

She sneered at them and around the circle. "Ottin, you can't stay silent. Join me and we'll take down this pup, now."

Ottin stood and shrugged out of a heavy cloak. If ever a one were to look like a fairy, it was Ottin. Regal in appearance, his clothing was neat and fastidious, his features symmetrical with a high brow, straight nose, and pointy chin. Shoulder-length pale brown hair was kept back by a thin silver circle crowning his brow.

"I think before I swear my court to a new king, I would want to know he was fey enough to rule."

He turned to the young man who earlier had shouted down Larin and held out his hand. The man retrieved a wooden box the size of a loaf of bread and handed it to Ottin. The Spring ruler faced Aleks and patted the box.

"One of the ways the well was kept hidden from us was with iron. We fey have a strong aversion to it. Do you? I have a piece of iron here in this box. I want you to pick it up."

Ottin brought the box to Aleks and lifted the lid, revealing a lump of cold iron. The unshaped rock looked harmless, but the crowd gasped, as if something deadly and poisonous like a viper had been revealed. Aleks had never had any trouble with iron before and so with a defiant look plunged his hand into the box and pulled out the hunk of ore.

To his surprise, his hand stung. He winced, but held on tight. Ottin noticed, however, and with a pleased smile gestured for Aleks to return the rock to the wooden box. He dropped it with haste, relieved to be done with it, his thoughts racing. Iron was harmless. This, this, this *superstition* was baseless. A piece of rock had no claim on him.

"You're fey enough for me," Ottin declared, closing the lid.

"You wretched piece of goblin breath," hissed Carita. "All of you. If you allow yourselves to be ruled by this pup, you deserve your fate. I will not bend a knee. Neither should you."

"Tell me more about this dragon," said Ottin, ignoring the steely fairy.

Aleks leaned back in the throne and steepled his fingers together, pressing his chin to them. "Fritjof has been attacking Niffleheim for some time now, presumably since Princess Zaria killed Koll."

"I heard that rumor," said Ottin. "Never did I let myself think it to be true, though. Are you saying she is the first not just to stop, but actually to destroy a dragon?"

"Yes," said Aleks.

His eyes lit up, and he scanned the crowd for Aleks' friends. "I'd like to meet her. Is she here?"

Henrik spoke up. "Zaria is here in Niffleheim, but this dragon business pulled her away."

"And yet you're all here," Ottin pointed out. "How dangerous could the situation be if you're here and she's... wherever she is?"

Christoffer rolled his eyes. "She's not alone. She's got a troll with her."

Geirr nodded. "You know how notoriously thick-skinned they are."

"Exactly," said Christoffer. "A troll makes for a great bodyguard."

"More to the point," Aleks said, reining in his friends. "This dragon situation requires us all to be on the same page. We must unite. We must do it now, and we must swear to uphold this alliance. We are all fey here, are we not?"

"Except your friends," said Carita.

"Fritjof nearly destroyed Niffleheim once," said Nori. "He's coming at us again."

It wasn't the name that people recognized but the story. Even Carita couldn't contain herself. She peeked nervously over her shoulder, as if the dragon in question was breathing down her neck. Only one dragon had ever tried to rip Niffleheim apart.

He had wormed his way to the fey realm by boring a hole from Jerndor. The dwarves' homes, tunnels, and businesses had been decimated, its people escaping to Malmdor through magic mirrors.

His sudden appearance in Niffleheim had thrown the courts into chaos and bloodshed. Brother fought against brother. Sister against sister. Parents against progeny. Every combination one could think of, fought – often to the death. Aleks watched as everyone at the Firething remembered this; those who were old enough to have been in those battles looked at each other, questions in their eyes.

"All our current troubles are from Fritjof," Nori confirmed for them. "Until recently, we were at relative peace."

"Your longest lasting," added Aleks. "Or so I'm told."

"We could trace our troubles back to you," Carita barked. "A changeling is to be killed on sight. Grimkell let you go."

Aleks dismissed her with a negligent wave. "My freedom was won in a way all of you can appreciate – with secrets, trickery, and skill."

"How do you explain this time?" she asked. "Why shouldn't we kill you now? Give me a reason not to."

He sat back in his throne, tapping his fingers against the arm. "How about I give you three. I beat my father at his own game. I won the challenges my aunt and uncle threw at me. The Lost Well bonded with me, and I control it."

"I call for a vote," said Sivert.

"You don't have the authority," shrieked Carita.

Ottin looked at her. "I think you'll find he does. You've been outmaneuvered."

"Where are Jelena and Rex?" she demanded. "They are not here to vote. Who rules Autumn? Without me, you're missing three of the courts' rulers."

"Ah, about that," said Aleks. "Sivert and I had to stop Jelena and Rex from attempting a coup with Grimkell. We caught him, and I'm sure we'll catch them soon enough. They've forfeited their rights to the Summer throne. I can install whomever I choose. As for Autumn, I rule it."

"I don't support your claim," she sneered.

"I don't need your support," Aleks retorted. "Grimkell, Cornelia, and Ytorm have fallen by my hand. Once I am king I will turn Grimkell over to the Firething's tender mercies. You can decide his fate."

"Grimkell did nothing wrong, he should be reinstated. You will never get my vote."

He nodded, having expected as much. "Then isn't it a good thing that I have Sivert's and I've appointed him acting ruler of Winter?"

She gasped in outrage. "I do not recognize your authority. He is not of noble blood, he can't rule even if you did have the authority... which you don't."

He raised an eyebrow. "Once I am crowned as king, my first order of business will be to ennoble Sivert and his house and promote him to ruler, not just acting ruler of Winter."

Carita stamped her foot. "I will not stand for this."

Ottin pushed her down, forcing her to sit. "Then you don't have to."

She snarled at him, but his Spring foxes leapt into action. Despite her struggles, they overpowered her, stilling her fight before Sivert ever had to get involved. The once regal and indomitable Winter ruler was brought low. She spat blood in his direction, letting it run down her chin as if it had been she who had eaten someone for lunch, and not been the one eaten.

In a span of minutes, from a series of unexpected events, a respected and strong leader was brought low. Aleks would take the lesson to heart and remember it always when dealing with the fey. Allies changed with the direction of the wind. The fight for dominance was swift and without mercy.

Those left standing, who still had a hat in the ring, would not give in so easily; they would play the game with him and see where it got them. Sivert, Saskia, and Nori were the only ones he could trust until he changed things down here.

"All those in favor of King Aleks?" asked Sivert, thumbing his dagger.

Nori raised her finger, casting the vote for Autumn. Most of the Autumn nobility followed suit. The witnesses behind them in the stands nudged those who had kept their hands down. Unable to resist the pressure, they too raised their hands.

Carita glared spitefully at her general as Sivert raised his hand. The soldiers all copied. Pragmatically, those behind them consented too, all the while gauging the reactions of their fallen ruler and new king.

Christoffer, Filip, Geirr, and Henrik raised their hands in solidarity. Aleks wasn't sure their votes counted, but he was grateful to them. That left two courts to vote. Would he ascend to the throne or would they descend into war over his claim? He looked between them, holding his breath in anticipation.

Leaderless, Summer cast their vote for Aleks, banking on his promise to spare them for their cooperation. It didn't hurt that he had Winter on his side, and that Winter had almost singlehandedly defeated them just a day earlier. It also didn't hurt that his promise of a reward to Winter had piqued several on that side's interest. Someone there would be maneuvering for a favor soon.

Ottin looked at his people, his back to Aleks, and raised his hand. Larin happily voted with him. The young man who'd spoken against him earlier grudgingly did the same. Soon, every hand was up in the Spring faction.

It was a damn miracle. The voting was unanimous with the exception of Carita and Grimkell; all four courts had spoken with one voice. Feeling almost sick to his stomach with relief, Aleks caught Saskia's admiring gaze and grinned. He wasn't dead, and his bid for kingship had been accepted.

"The ayes have it," said Sivert, lowering his hand. "Let's get you crowned, lad."

Chapter Twelve: The Trofast Blessing

The Firething turned into a coronation in a blink of an eye, astounding the Summer and Spring courts who had thought there'd be more time for planning and politicking, and perhaps even some backstabbing. Nori had thought of everything, which astounded Aleks. When had she the time to organize anything let alone everything? With Sivert backing up her plans the transition had been flawless.

He felt jittery waiting for everything to start. Nori elbowed him, causing him to flinch, but he hadn't the focus to tell her to back off. Instead, his gaze gravitated toward Saskia, finding her next to her father near the thrones. Her smile soothed his inner turmoil. The scene was almost set.

Staked into the ground, banners from the Autumn Court encircled the crowd in fluttering red and blue fabric, reminding everyone – as if they needed any reminding – which court would be ruling at the end of this coronation.

Small fires were lit in bronze braziers and scattered amongst the stones, casting the fey in shades of orange and red. Nori instructed several fairies carrying large piles of wood to leave their offerings at the side. A bonfire would be lit in the center of the Firething after Aleks' acceptance of duty and crowning. She'd insisted that a celebration would be necessary before there be any more maneuverings on their part.

"We must give them a coronation to remember," Nori hissed. "Don't mess it up."

He made a face at her. "You don't mess it up."

She sniffed. "Very mature."

"He knows what to do," Filip said, pushing Aleks along. "He just hates being the center of attention."

"I know what *he's* supposed to do, but what are we supposed to do?" asked Geirr.

"Keep him from puking up his lunch," said Christoffer.

"Just relax," Henrik said, flanking him and helping the others to lead him away.

Aleks glanced over his shoulder multiple times as his friends led him outside through the giant monoliths. All this runaround seemed nuts just so he could make a second entrance and follow the traditions laid out by the previous royals. It was ostentatious and unnecessary, but Nori and Sivert had insisted on all the pomp.

Outside the Firething, Aleks paced, feeling both anxious and impatient. Beside him, Henrik narrated the scene and gently reminded Aleks what was expected of him. Most of what he said buzzed around him like the hum of a heater in the midst of winter, and though he listened, he heard very little.

Canvassing the scene, Aleks noted the path he would take to the thrones had been lined with flowers, as Spring quickly jumped onboard with Nori's and Sivert's plans, acting as if they had been in partnership all along. It was a clever positioning move from Ottin to place Summer as the low-man on the totem pole.

Not to be left behind, Summer provided music. Bone flutes, wooden panpipes, sweet piccolos, and other enchanted woodwinds sparked to life, painting the air with a tapestry of sounds. It arrested Aleks mid-pace, and he gulped. Never would he forget the moving beauty of it, as it sent shivers up his spine. The giants in Jerndor would beg and weep tears just to listen to a recording of it.

The final transformation to the space came from four fairies — two Winter, and two Autumn. The Winter fey coated one throne in ice, sending frost into the grass. The Autumn fey gilded the larger throne in liquid gold. It slid over the chair legs and flowed through the grass like molten lava. Onward raced both rivers of fire and ice, gold and silver, until they stopped suddenly on either side of the giant stones where he stood.

"It's really happening," said Geirr, gingerly touching the golden side with his toe, watching it ripple.

"It is," confirmed Henrik, leaning against the megalith. "You're going to do marvelous things for Niffleheim, Aleks. You are exactly what this place needs."

Christoffer clapped him on the back. "This makes three of my friends crowned royalty. If only I could tell the ladies back home, they'd be all over me in a heartbeat."

Filip toed the frosted side, watching the grass crack and break off. Quietly, he asked, "You won't forget about us will you? You'll still be Aleks when this is all over, right?"

Aleks knew his friend asked this not only of himself, but of Zaria and Henrik. The Stag Lord sensed this too, and placing a hand on Filip's shoulder said, "We'll always be ourselves. Neither the job nor power will define us."

Eyes troubled, Filip gestured around and said, "She wouldn't have missed this for the world."

"She'll pull through and be herself again," Henrik said. "I did and so will she."

Aleks hummed in agreement. "Zaria is the strongest of us. She'll come back to us... to you."

Filip flashed a wan smile just as Nori appeared and shoved her way through the group. Briskly she arranged everyone, putting Christoffer in front, Filip next, Geirr, Henrik, herself, and then Aleks. Saskia wasn't part of the procession; she'd wait with her father until Aleks formally declared alliance to the other courts.

Nori gave Henrik a sword with amber buttons, inset like eyes, in a carved bone pummel shaped like a raven's head. Aleks wasn't one for swords, but he nearly salivated at the sight of it. Henrik would present this to him. The ceremonial gesture would show the courts that the outside world was ready to accept Niffleheim and its king.

His sister held a matching crown of entwined amber and bone, carved to look like leaves and feathers—a symbol of power he would gladly accept. Seeing it, Aleks realized how much his relationship with his sister had changed. All lingering bitterness melted like snowbanks in bright sunshine. He had to swallow around a lump that suddenly formed in his throat. Nori was a pretty great sister.

He touched the crown. "Thanks," he murmured.

"You're welcome," she said.

For only being with each other a short period of time, she knew him very well. Nori found the symbol of power to give him that he would gladly accept. It represented Autumn, but more importantly it represented him – it represented Airi. There wasn't another crown for him.

There wasn't another raven for that matter. He scanned the skies overhead for her. Without Airi the scene wasn't complete, but he had no idea when she would return and neither he, Nori, nor the rest of Niffleheim would wait on her arrival. It was time.

As the music took on a new flair, bright and triumphant – a processional fit for a fey king – Nori shoved Christoffer through the megaliths. He stumbled. Throwing a quick glare over his shoulder, he straightened, smiled, and marched ahead. Filip and Geirr followed, and Aleks had to suppress a nervous chuckle as Filip pressed ahead with a lordly tilt to his chin. He looked faintly ridiculous, though Aleks supposed it was meant to look knightly. His friend was just too gangly to pull it off.

Geirr's walk was everything Filip's wasn't. It bore a noble sheen to it that Aleks could only hope to emulate when it was his turn. His stomach churned unpleasantly, and he pressed a hand to it. Henrik clapped him reassuringly on the shoulder and walked through the megaliths, following the path set by the others. The presence of the Stag Lord was noted by all in attendance.

Nori bounced on the balls of her feet. "Six, seven, eight –"

"What are you doing?"

"Counting his steps," she retorted.

"Whatever for?" Aleks asked, completely baffled.

"Shh," she hissed. "Thirteen, fourteen, and fifteen."

She started walking. Wildly Aleks wondered if he needed to count to fifteen, too, before heading out. He decided he didn't care to count. It seemed better for him to go when she finished her walk, so he watched and waited from the wings.

As he took his first step toward the Firething's entrance, a welcomed "Eye-riii!" rent the air. Aleks' gaze found Airi immediately. She sailed over the megalith and landed on his head. Definitely not the dignified look he was aiming for. He reached up to pull her off, but she pecked his fingers.

"Ouch," he muttered. "What did you do that for?"

"Ravagers," she croaked.

He tried again, but her beak snapped, catching his thumb. He cursed and nursed it. "What about them? What did King Flein say?"

"Coming."

"King Flein is coming?" asked Aleks. "That's good. We can talk and settle this."

She knocked his head. "Coming. Coming. Coming," she repeated.

"All right, all right, enough," Aleks said, pulling her off his head and settling her on his shoulder. "Let's get through this ceremony and then I'll meet him as equals when he arrives. Okay?"

"No." She nipped his ear, causing him to flinch.

"Stop that," he warned.

"Dummy," she cawed, gripping his shoulder tighter with her talons.

He grimaced, but forced himself to start walking. As he passed through the entrance she cawed, "Dummy!" and launched away, clipping the side of his head with her wings.

Well there went his grand entrance, he thought sourly, fighting off an embarrassed blush. Had he really wanted her present? What had he been thinking? He watched her wheel around in the sky and dive, making her way to Saskia. The Winter fairy looked surprised, but offered a hand to the white raven. Traitorous bird. Wasn't she his white raven?

He caught Nori's eye, she looked to be twitching. Whether it was in irritation or mirth he couldn't tell and it was probably best not to ask. He already felt enough of a fraud. Taking a deep breath, he squared his shoulders and gritted his teeth. One step at a time. One foot in front of the other. He could do this.

Aleks nodded to the musicians as he passed them, silently thanking them for their uninterrupted playing. He wound his way along the path, passing the flower girls from Summer. He gave them a small bow. One of them blushed. His gaze caught Nori's again, and she looked like she was proud of him.

His confidence soared, and he kept going. He came to Sivert, Saskia, and his traitorous raven next. He stopped beside them. "Sir," he started.

"Son," the general said, clasping his forearm. "Wolves will turn on their own. Show no weakness."

"Yes, sir," Aleks said.

"Dummy," Airi croaked.

"Shh," hushed Saskia, soothing down Airi's ruffled feathers. As Aleks turned to go, he was halted by a soft, "Wait." At his questioning look, she gestured to a large bundle of fabric and fur in her arms. "May I?"

Shaking out the fabric, Saskia presented a Winter cloak, long, white and bordered with taupe-colored bear fur. It glimmered with bronze threads, stitched to reveal a scene featuring a bear, a fox, a deer, and a raven in a snow-covered forest. It was fit for a conquering Norse king, and Aleks guessed it could only have been made with magic. Someone in the Winter Court was a true seamstress, or had made a trip to Granny's in Jerndor for her magic-laced sewing tools.

She indicated he was to wear it over his own clothes. Aleks nodded eagerly. He'd feel more like a king wearing this. She smiled and walked around him, laying it over his shoulders. She smoothed out the wrinkles and stepped back beside her father. He could still feel the press of her hands.

He cleared his throat. "Thanks."

"Family," said Airi, staring beadily at the cloak. "In danger. Family."

"Don't worry, Airi," Saskia said. "We'll protect each other."

Then she pressed a kiss to his cheek, flooding him with so much warmth Aleks had to make a concerted effort not to transform. She branded him with her kiss, a sign for all to see that he allied with Winter, and with Sivert, but in particular with her.

He wasn't even mad at that, because she branded herself as his, too. Tipping his head, he caught her lips in a soft buttery kiss that melted into another one. She was the one blushing when he pulled back. He chucked her under the chin and after one last breath-stealing kiss, turned away.

Passing his court next, Aleks made eye contact with each and every member. In their midst, surrounded by a hulking guard, Grimkell glowered like a heavy thundercloud, his hands bound behind his back. Aleks caught his hate-filled gaze and held it, forcing his birth father to acknowledge him. He sneered in contempt, but for Aleks it was enough. They both knew who had won.

He continued on until he came abreast his sister and friends. Nori's vulpine features sharpened in victory as she took him by the shoulders and turned him to face her. Her smile was so wide it flashed every fang in her head – a gesture not for his benefit, but for their audience. He fisted his hands tightly and shook them out, releasing built up nerves.

The music stopped on an upward lilting trill, not unlike birdsong, and Nori raised the hand not holding the crown. The crowd stilled to hear what she said. "Today we crown a king. Today we crown my brother Aleks. His story is one for song and legend. These are his triumphs and achievements:

"He is the first fey to find the Lost Well, hidden for nearly a thousand years. Not only did he find it, he bonded with it. If you need proof of this, remember that as a changeling he should have lost his powers, but instead, they are increasing in number and strength.

"My brother has reunited old alliances with the ellefolken and the sorceresses. Aligned by their side, he helped not just to defeat, but to kill a dragon. Koll is no more a threat in this world, nor in any other because of him."

Aleks almost protested this, but Nori's meaningful glare kept him silent. She continued, "Our new king has outwitted our father, Grimkell, a most formidable opponent. When Grimkell tried to reclaim his rule of the Autumn Court, he lost to Aleks.

"Our relatives, Aunt Cornelia, Uncle Ytorm, cousins Isak and Eskil tried to bind my brother to them, but he fooled them, too. He won the unwinnable trials."

At the crowd's gasp, she caught their gazes. "Yes, those trials. He escaped the oubliette, crossed the inland sea, befriended an enormous water-wyvern, gained the heart of a white raven, and fought off a shortage of Ravagers."

"A what?" exclaimed Aleks, alarmed.

"Did she just say a shortage of Ravagers — for dwarves? Really?" muttered Christoffer. "What collective noun will we have next? A gossip of giants? A beauty of hags? A doom of dragons?"

"That one's actually a devastation of dragons," said Henrik.

Nori pressed on, speaking above them. "These are just the things I know about. He's done what no other could do. He's done the impossible. Just imagine to what great heights he'll take Niffleheim. We are most eager for his wisdom. We are eager for his reign. With Aleks we will soar!"

The enthralled crowd hung on every word she spoke. His resume, as she put it, was long and filled with accomplishments nobody else had been able to do. But it was all a sham.

He didn't find the well. It was Hector who had led them there. He didn't bond with the well. The well bonded to him – all because Airi dropped his stargazer into its depths, and fool that he was, he took it back.

How could he claim his friend's deeds? It was Zaria who fought Koll and won, not him. He'd been fighting and failing against Koll's brothers. If he'd been better then, maybe Fritjof wouldn't be loose now. He held his tongue though, on the hope that going through this coronation would help him raise an army to fight the dragon of chaos.

As for the other adulations Nori had heaped upon him, they didn't hold much weight, either. Not when one looked closely. He'd beaten Grimkell only because the fairy hadn't known he was part of the bargain with Zaria on that first trip through Niffleheim.

And his aunt and uncle? He hadn't been alone in the trials. In fact, if he'd listened to Airi sooner when he was trapped in the oubliette, he wouldn't have been racing against the clock and almost losing everything in the last few minutes. Filip and Geirr actually provided the most valuable contributions to win the trials with their savvy and logic.

Worse still, he hadn't fought off a horde… a shortage of ravenous Ravagers – that was Zaria. She'd given up her freedom to save them. It was she who was suffering the consequences. He'd only found her again because of a wish on the well, which hadn't turned out that great either, what with those possessed dwarves coming along with the wish.

He shuffled his feet and hissed, "Let's move along, okay? We've got to finish things here and come up with a plan to defeat Fritjof."

Nori turned to Henrik and motioned for him to come closer. "My fellow fey, may I formally introduce to you Henrik, Stag Lord of the ellefolken, and Aleks' particular friend. He is here to give a gift and a blessing to our king."

Henrik gripped the sword and examined its bone and amber design. He rubbed the top of the raven's head on the pummel. Gazing out at the enrapt crowd, he spoke aloud, pitching his voice so that it carried with deep resonance allowing everyone to hear him.

"Aleks Mickelsen, you are the king the rest of the realms have long desired to see seated on the Fox Throne. You are wise and kind, you are loyal and strong. No other qualities could attract to you such a pure creature as a white raven.

"You are the hope of Niffleheim. You are its brightest star. This beautiful sword, represents our hopes for your kingship. It is called Trofast, meaning faithful. May your reign be long and be marked by unfailing faithfulness between you and your subjects, and between Niffleheim and Elleken."

Henrik, balancing the sword across his palms, extended it to Aleks. He picked it up, and felt the weight of his solemn duty. "I accept your blessing and gift. In return, I pledge that so long as I am king, Niffleheim will be as this sword – strong, earnest, and true."

Nori lifted up the matching crown. Aleks knelt on one knee. "This crown is called the Ráfi Crown. It is a sign of peace. May it bless your rule. May peace always rest upon your head and crown your days."

Aleks swore, "Peace will be the hallmark of my reign. It will be for all of Niffleheim. No threat of chaos can assail us as we unite in one purpose."

It started with a single yip that grew as more foxes and fairies joined in, until Nori had to silence them again. As she began to lower the crown over his head, she asked, "Do you promise to honor our ways, to uphold every court as an equal, to be just and fair in all your dealings, and to use the power of the well wisely?"

"I promise," he said.

"And will you vow always to put the fate of Niffleheim above the fate of yourself, or the fates of your friends, allies, and family?"

Aleks licked his lips, uncertain. In the space of that brief hesitation a single wail rent the air. The sound was not one of excitement like before, but one of terror and fear. It startled both Nori and him and she let the crown go. It plunked down around his ears, and he had only the time to massage one of them when another cry split the scene.

He tried to pin down the source, when Henrik's arm cut in front of him. "There, in the back," cried the Stag Lord.

Aleks saw where he pointed. A disturbance pushed against the Spring Court and they were resisting. Magic blossomed and filled the air as the Spring nobles began to return fire.

Christoffer asked, "What's going on?"

"Dwarves," replied Henrik.

"Ravagers," agreed Nori, drawing a blade. "We have to stop them."

"I don't have my bow," protested Aleks.

Henrik pointed to the new blade on his hip. "Needs must, my friend. Abandon the bow and arrow for the sword. You'll need it."

"I'm not interested in close combat," Aleks muttered, drawing the glimmering Trofast blade. He gave it a practice swing, getting used to the feel of it.

"But you are prepared for it," Nori replied. "We just didn't anticipate an outside enemy. We thought one of the other courts would try to stop your coronation."

Aleks was indeed prepared for a coup attempt. His armor lay underneath his shirt. He only lacked his helmet.

"Dummy," cried Airi, flying by and clipping his head.

Saskia appeared in front of him with her icy blades. "Why does she keep calling you a dummy?"

"Because she tried to warn me the Ravagers were coming," Aleks huffed, annoyed. Why did he always understand what she meant after it was too late to do anything about it?

"Of course she did," Nori sniffed. "I'll repeat it again, Airi's wasted on you."

"Like you could do any better," Aleks retorted hotly. "I though she meant King Flein was coming."

Nori shook her head. "Thoroughly, perfectly, totally, and utterly wasted."

Chapter Thirteen: The Eighth Fox Throne War

The fighting kindled in the Spring stands, as they battled on their own. The Ravagers were vicious, stabbing, biting, and clawing their way forward – attacking as if possessed. They probably were. Aleks had seen it happen, but then only one at a time. What about the dwarves he'd captured? Was Hertha still possessed? Did Fritjof grow stronger? Whatever was going on, it wasn't good.

"This is the final battle," Nori pronounced grimly.

Sivert shook his head. "This is just the first push. We'll hold them off."

Saskia looked between them both. "One of you is wrong."

"I'm never wrong," Sivert said. "Not about fighting."

Nori and Aleks exchanged a look that spoke volumes, because of the two, Aleks wouldn't bet against Nori. Before they could say anything, a new figure appeared in the crowd. One whose presence made Aleks' blood boil.

Floki, that rotten dwarf prince, was riding in on an armored bear. Somehow he was free and here; someone had set him loose. Most likely Brunhild, as she joined him riding her own bear, or Frigga her faithful scout, who was also mounted. They must have arrived by way of the Thief of Peace's Passage. It was time to do damage control.

The women in league with Floki roared with renewed vigor and swarmed the Spring stands like flies at a picnic table. Summer hung back watching, preparing to join only if it affected them and that made Aleks seethe. Were they not all fairies? Were they not all on the same side?

"Help them," he shouted. "Don't just stand there. Help them!"

Christoffer took out his daggers, twirling them. "I'm ready for some payback."

"For Zaria," agreed Filip, drawing his short blade into his hand.

Geirr changed grips on his sword. "For Zaria!"

The three charged off the dais, only to have Sivert catch them. He hauled them back up where they started, depositing them like naughty children. "Don't get in my way," he warned them.

"Are you kidding me?" whined Christoffer. "Where's the fun in that?"

Sivert ignored his outburst, his keen mind busily analyzing the threats. The general turned aside to bark orders at waiting attendants, who ran on nimble feet to deliver them to the troops. The war machine that was Winter sprang into action like well-oiled bits and bobs. Each had their own role to play, and each used their special gifts to lend strength to their brothers and sisters at arms.

Icy walls sprang up from the ground, dividing the Ravagers from the Spring Court and blocking their attacks. Snowballs the size of small avalanches hurtled forward, smashing dwarves to the ground. Ice frosted the ground beneath their feet, sending them flying sideways.

It didn't matter, as the dwarves changed direction with as nimble a war machine as Winter. Floki and Brunhild bellowed orders from the safety of the rear line. In an instant, the Ravagers went from close combat to range. Spears which had been used to stab opponents now lobbed over the walls where they rained down upon Summer, Autumn, and Spring, creating chaos in their ranks.

Sivert retaliated by sending in a new team. Frostbite developed on tips of toes and ends of noses. Hands froze on spears, pitching dwarves forward when they found they couldn't let go. Summer finally joined the fight, but caused more problems, for they flung out magic in every direction, heedless of who they were actually fighting. Many of their attacks did more harm to Autumn than they did to the dwarves.

"They're using the dwarves to come for the throne," Filip observed. "We could really use Zaria now."

Aleks wholeheartedly agreed, but she was still suffering the effects of the dwarvish chains. To free her, they had to reclaim the Drakeland Sword. Its current owner, however, was unlikely to give it up. Floki waved it over his head like a beacon – a taunting one. That sword, however, put a big target on his head.

"That's the Drakeland Sword," shouted Geirr, excitedly. He looked to Aleks and Nori. "But why does he have it?"

"Isn't it obvious? The lieutenant used it to free him from his father's prison and then gifted it to him," said Nori, with a bitter bite to her words.

"We have to get it back," said Filip with fervor, finding his purpose in all of this. "It's the only way to save Zaria."

"We'll get it," promised Henrik, feeling the same urgency as Filip.

The Autumn Court reared back, hissing and spitting like a defanged snake. They trampled themselves, as they tried to escape Summer's attacks. One-by-one they were knocked down and out, for most of Autumn's heavy fighters, were either missing or imprisoned.

Grimkell smirked from his position in the middle and raised his bound hands to a cowering, matronly fairy. She looked up, seeing her former ruler, and knowing how powerful he was, decided to take her chances. She reached out for him with shaking hands.

"NO!" shouted Nori, seeing the inevitable and trying to stop it; but, truth magic isn't a weapon one can wield like the wind. She couldn't topple her opponents with it – at least not physically.

The woman never glanced over, she didn't think twice, and Grimkell, his father and enemy, was free in a trice. Powerful winds kicked up immediately, batting away every incoming spear, tree limb, vine, icicle, and fireball. They hurtled off course, into the backs of unsuspecting Spring.

"Don't fight each other," snarled Aleks, clenching his fists. "We have to stop the dwarves."

Airi pealed from above, dodging a spear spinning wildly through the air. "Eighth war. Eighth war."

Geirr nudged him. "Did your bird just say –"

"Eighth war?" finished Aleks. "Yes. Damn it."

"Did you really expect anything less?" asked Saskia.

"No," muttered Aleks, utterly disgusted. "My father is too opportunistic to miss a chance like this, and he won't let Summer get the victory."

Nori sniffed, menacingly, "When I get my hands on the fairy who set him free, she'll rue the day she was born."

Sivert stared at the scene, his mind calculating and processing everything as fast as it was happening. "We must win this assault from the dwarves, and subdue all comers for your throne. You are not to leave my side, do you hear?"

Then he ordered a wall of Winter fey to stand between the fight and the thrones. Several Autumn fey plunged toward them, seeking safety, but Winter held them off, not knowing who was a friend. Aleks wanted to give the order to let them through, but held his tongue, knowing Sivert didn't need or want the distraction.

Airi landed on Aleks' shoulder, watching the dwarves pit themselves against ice and snow, vine and thorn, rain and mud, song and sound, fang and fire. So many fairies were caught up in the fight, most didn't know who to attack. As much as they found their true marks, they egged each other on by fighting themselves. Floki and Brunhild thrived on the ensuing chaos, which, in turn, no doubt fueled Fritjof.

Slowly, the chaos was wrangled into some semblance of order and control. With the Winter fairies calling to the courts, relaying Sivert's orders, the battle seemed to turn, as fey who before were attacking blindly, now attacked in accord with Sivert's vision, for they understood how powerful his own gift could be. Floki blustered and bellowed, but even Brunhild was on the retreat, forced to give ground to the Winter march.

It was then that Aleks realized he'd paid too much attention to the battle roiling closer to him and his friends, and had lost track of Grimkell. He searched wildly for him, but with the seething, teeming turmoil of battle on all sides, it was like looking for a needle in a haystack. There was too much movement, and strangely, eerily, no wind.

"What's wrong?" Saskia asked, noticing his sudden withdrawal.

Gripping Saskia's shoulder, he scoured the field for a tall, graying man. "Where did Grimkell go?"

"He's over there!" shouted Filip, thrusting his finger in the fey's direction.

Grimkell tossed aside a group of Winter fey, who realized too late that the dangerous Autumn prisoner was free. He then cut a swath through the fey around him as if they were nothing but bothersome gnats. He surged forward to find his allies, and in a blink of the eye Carita found him, appearing like a stranger through heavy fog. It didn't take a witch to predict that alliance.

Together, the two did something that Aleks' couldn't quite catch. The fog seemed to swallow them up and spit them out wherever it chose. Each time they appeared, a new fey stood with them and then they disappeared again. One from Summer, one from Autumn, two from Spring, one from Winter. Over and over, until Aleks knew without question his father would press for the throne. Today. Now.

"Carita is using her gifts," noted Saskia beside him. She gasped, covering her mouth. "Oh no!"

Sivert glowered, and hurled a dagger to the ground by his feet. "She got Bendix to join them. That man has a silver tongue. May he rot. I was counting on him for our side. This changes things."

Geirr asked, "Who's Bendix? His powers wouldn't be timing magnetos would it?"

Nori looked at him despairingly. "I don't know what a magneto is, but Bendix is a dangerous Spring fairy. He could cause ice to burn, rocks to melt, and clouds to hurl themselves to the ground like anvils."

"And convince doddering old men that he's with them to the end," Sivert ground out.

"You're not doddering," Saskia protested.

"I might as well be," he said. "My gift has never acted up on me like this before. I always know my allies and my strategy. Always."

"It's Fritjof," said Aleks. "He's been doing the same to me and my gifts."

He turned to Aleks. "Son, I know I said you needed to stay by me, but I have had a change of heart. If we can't trust our gifts, we can't trust ourselves. You all need to get out of here."

"Why?" asked Filip. "Wouldn't it still be safer here?"

Sivert shook his head, and began herding them behind the thrones. "With Bendix on Grimkell's side, I can't count on any fey staying on ours. Not even my most loyal soldiers. Don't trust any fey except your sister, my daughter, and me. Saskia, you know what I need you to do."

"Yes, father," she said meekly.

"Protect me?" guessed Aleks.

She nodded. "You're the hope of so many down here." She paused and then added, "You're my hope."

"Right, then," said Aleks, too focused to be embarrassed, even by Christoffer's kissy sounds in the background. He plucked the coin from his pocket and held it tight, wishing fervently for the safety of his friends and allies. It disappeared. Now he had none.

He sheathed his sword and grabbed her hand in his and ran. Christoffer stopped poking fun and started after them, Geirr and Nori right behind. Henrik and Filip sprinted after them. Following his gut, Aleks weaved in and out of the stones, circling behind the field, taking his friends up and over a half dozen small hills.

"Where to now?" asked Christoffer, panting as they crested the last one and wound this way and that toward the Autumn Court.

"We get the Drakeland Sword," said Aleks. "It's our best chance at getting out of this alive."

"But how?" asked Christoffer.

"The Lost Well," Aleks explained. "I need a coin."

"Will it be open?" asked Filip, putting on speed.

Henrik hefted his sword. "There should be one or two coins in the hallway."

Aleks grinned. "Exactly."

"Coin. Get coin," croaked Airi. "Coin."

Nori clapped him on the back. "Maybe you're not so useless after all, baby brother."

He rolled his eyes. "Come on, everyone!"

They hurtled over hills, skipped down vales, and navigated rocky paths. Winding their way around the courts, Aleks took them up the hill to the plains' entrance and transformed, leaving Geirr to carry his sword, and Henrik to pick up his crown as he leapt through it in his dash to the opening.

Fleet-footed, he raced Saskia and Nori through the underground cavern. Airi swooped overhead, keeping watch. She flew back and forth between the humans and the foxes, guiding his bipedal friends, until Aleks rounded the corner, out of sight, but not out of breath.

Once in the corridor, Aleks scoured the ground, using his keen fox vision to spy the dusty coins. Wedged in the far corner, where the hallway dead-ended, a single coin waited. He shifted back to his human form. Using the fading vestiges of light from his transformation, he plucked up the coin and held it aloft to his followers.

His grin was triumphant. "Found one," he said. "But before I make the wish, you two might want to switch back. The last time I summoned with the well not only did I get what I wished – Zaria – but I also got some tagalongs."

"You're expecting Floki," Saskia said, standing upright. She formed deadly icicles in her hands. They glittered with sharp intent.

He nodded, rubbing dirt off the coin. "Brunhild, too. She might be close enough to him to see it happen and grab onto him."

Nori frowned. "Shouldn't we wait for your friends? It's not like you or I have any weapons."

Aleks grumbled, "Why can't we transform and keep our weapons?"

"Oh, Fiona can," Nori said. "Probably nature's way of making up for the fact that she drops them half the time. Be glad you can navigate instead."

"We're here," Airi trilled out, 'flying' down the hall on an antlered perch.

Henrik ignored her presence on his hood with the kind of resignation Aleks felt when she did something he knew he couldn't change. "Did it work?" he asked, peering around.

Filip, right behind him, raced over. "Did you get the sword?"

"I haven't made the wish yet," Aleks admitted. "We're waiting for everyone to arrive."

"We thought we'd need more backup," explained Saskia, indicating her icicles and their lack of weapons.

Panting, Geirr came to a stop beside Filip. He handed Aleks his crown and weapons. "Carry these yourself next time, would you? I'm not your squire," he complained.

"No, that's Filip's role," joked Christoffer.

"Hurry up and make the wish," Nori said impatiently.

Aleks squeezed the coin in his fist, closed his eyes and wished hard for the Drakeland Sword. A flash of light broke the gloom and an angry dwarf on top of an even angrier bear, snarled, "WILL YOU SLAUGHTER THEM ALREADY! THEY'RE NOTHING BUT A BUNCH OF PUSSYFOOTING, ROTTEN, FOUL-BREATHED GHOUL BOOGIES –"

Henrik pressed his sword against Floki's throat, cutting off the dwarf mid-rant. The dwarf looked to his left and right and saw he was pressed tightly against the walls. Stuck as they were, he and his bear weren't going anywhere.

Henrik towered menacingly over the prince. "I'll take back that sword. Let go."

At the sound of Henrik's voice, and the sight of those around him, Floki relaxed his rigid posture. Wetting his lips he said cajolingly, "Hart –"

"That's Stag Lord now," the ellefolken prince said silkily. "Hand over the sword."

Floki gripped it tighter, so Aleks stuck the tip of his sword against the dwarf's stomach. "I believe my friend said to hand it over."

The dwarf's voice went up a notch. "You're Princess Zaria's little friend… Albert, wasn't it?"

"Aleks," he corrected. "King Aleks of Niffleheim. The sword."

The moment the dwarf prince's grip relaxed, Filip snatched the Drakeland Sword away with a shout of joy. "Let's free Zar-Zar!"

"You won't win, even if you free the little sorceress," Floki sneered. "She won't defeat Fritjof."

Henrik nicked the dwarf's neck, halting whatever else he was going to say. "Princess Zaria's already eliminated the oldest dragon in existence. What's one more to her?"

Floki laughed. "You think a little bit of magic can stop him? He's always been the most powerful brother. I should have aligned with him in the beginning."

Disgusted, Geirr said, "Your father spared you. He clearly sees something in you, but what, I have no idea, and he obviously loves you. Why do you insist on following this path?"

"You won't get a good response from him," said Nori. "He's too far gone. Too in love with the idea of power to give it up now."

"What are we going to do with him?" asked Geirr.

"We'll toss him in the dungeons. King Flein will want to trade back for him. We can use him to broker peace," said Aleks with a certainty he didn't feel, but not seeing a better plan.

"Dumb plan," croaked Airi, preening her feathers. "Need better one."

"It's all I got," said Aleks. "Anybody got a better one?" They all shook their heads. "All right, then. After locking him up, we get Zaria and Zorka."

"Then what?" asked Filip, already angling toward the Autumn Court, eager to reunite with Zaria.

"Then we go knock on Fritjof's door," Aleks said.

"Again," knocked Airi.

Christoffer pouted, "That's my joke."

Floki jerked on the reins of his bear, and the creature snarled in pain, rearing up and knocking Henrik back. He fell against the walls, his sword clattering to the ground. Startled, Airi launched into the air, and did the most brilliant thing Aleks could think of – she let loose a giant poop, and to his eternal delight, it plopped directly on the berserking dwarf's face.

"Bullseye!" crowed Christoffer.

"I'll feed you bacon every day for the rest of your life," Nori promised. "Come, be my raven."

"Stop trying to steal Airi," Aleks retorted. "She's mine."

"You're mine," Airi cawed back.

"Should I be jealous?" asked Saskia, amused.

"You're both my girls," he said, giving her a quick buss on the mouth.

The angry dwarf spluttered and gagged and scrubbed at his face, wiping the poop into his beard. Henrik hauled Floki off the bear and shoved him to the ground. Saskia and Filip worked together to tie him up, while Henrik soothed the wounded animal, removing the cruel bit. Eventually the bear quieted down and with gentle leading, Henrik maneuvered the beast out of the corridor and out into the open plains.

Aleks and the others dragged Floki to his feet and shoved him along behind the pair. Airi circled above, keeping watch. It was a grand moment for Aleks, sweeping back through the plains and out into the heart of Niffleheim. They all talked excitedly, riding the rush of victory.

Din and smoke rising to view from the Firething, gave them all pause. "We have to take him down," Aleks said, referring to Fritjof. "It's the only way to stop this war."

"How do you know?" asked Geirr.

"I don't," said Aleks, grimly.

"Well, I do," said Nori, flinging a strand of hair behind her face. "To stop chaos in its tracks –"

"We've got to stop it at its source," finished Henrik.

Saskia smiled viciously. "I'm ready to put this dwarf and dragon on ice."

The streets of Autumn Court were empty, but not like before when it felt deserted and everyone hid to protect themselves from conflicting forces within the court. Signs of repair were already underway with scaffolding going up on this building and that, and much of the rubble cleared away.

The silence now was more impatient and expectant, less fearful and timid. Most of the fey from Autumn were either at the Firething or nearby trying to gain glimpses of Aleks' coronation.

More activity took place inside the palace. Aleks heard Zorka before he saw her. She was arguing with a teenage fairy girl sporting red and purple hair over who had the better hair coloring recipe. Spying them from the corner of her eye, Zorka turned to greet them.

"King already?" she asked, grinning toothily. "That went faster than I thought it would."

"He's king all right, but we've got problems," said Geirr, stepping aside and revealing a battered Prince Floki.

"Ravagers," agreed Airi with a chirrup.

"Ravagers attacked?" Zorka asked, pouting. "I wanted another go at them."

"You'll get your chance," said Aleks. "But first we've got to take down a dragon."

She rubbed her hands together. "That's more like it. After this I will be telling all the good war stories around the bonfires. Kanutte is going to be spitting nails. Have I told you recently how glad I am you brought me here?"

Nori caught Zorka up, as Aleks and the others went to get Zaria and bring her down. Filip carried the Drakeland Sword like a conquering war hero bringing a prize to his beloved maiden. He strode through the bedchamber door and over to her bed. They all crowded behind him.

"Zar-Zar," he said, joyfully, waving it in the air. "Wake up! We've got the sword."

She struggled to open her eyes. "Filip?"

"Hey," he whispered, stroking her cheek. "We got back the Drakeland Sword. You're going to be all right."

She licked her parched lips. "You got the sword?" she whispered.

"We really did," he said, beaming. "Hold out your hands and I'll cut these chains off you."

Feebly she lifted her hands, and he aligned the sword carefully between her palms. One quick slice upward and the chain broke apart into a thousand tiny gemstones. They rained everywhere, pinging off the bed, floors, and walls, bouncing off knees, shins, and shoes. Everyone held their breath as Filip untangled the remaining chain and tossed it to the floor. He hauled Zaria into his arms and hugged her tight, his eyes suspiciously wet.

"How are you feeling?" he asked, stroking her hair.

"Still finding it hard to breathe," she wheezed, jokingly, and wrapped her arms around his waist.

"Oh!" he exclaimed, jumping back and breaking her hold.

She inhaled sharp and deep. Life came back to her eyes. Magic, too, as they glowed a bright purple, like a thousand neon lights. She chaffed her arms and rubbed her hands together. A minute later she held a tiny purple fireball in her hand. It was smaller than a marble. Closing her fist she snuffed it out.

"Hmm, not quite what I was going for with that."

"You need a little while to recover, but you're already on the mend," Henrik said.

She nodded, flexing her hands. Impulsively, she threw her arms around Filip and kissed him. "Thank you,

Filip," she said, and beaming tiredly at the others, added, "Thank you all for saving me."

"It's good to have you back," Christoffer said, pulling her from Filip's hold. "We've missed you."

"It's good to be back. I missed me, too."

"Hey," Christoffer complained. "I tell the jokes around here."

"I've missed you, too," she amended, contritely. "I've missed you all." A yawn caught up with her then, and Filip rushed to settle her back against the pillows.

"You need to rest," he told her. "We should call for a brownie."

She yawned again, but determinedly kept her eyes open. "Not yet. What's happening with Fritjof and the Ravagers?"

So they told her. All of it and more besides. When they were done she pursed her lips. "Sounds like I've got a dragon to take down. One way or another, he'll go the way of Koll."

"We're a team," Aleks said. "You're not in this alone."

Those were words to remember later.

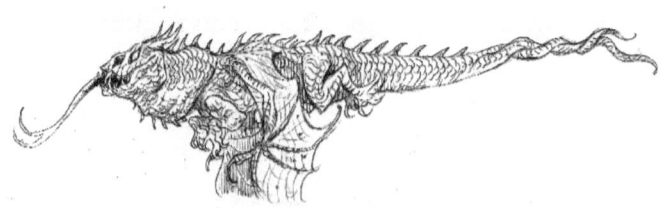

Chapter Fourteen: Combating Chaos

"Oh, great. You're here," Aleks growled at his father, who, a short while later, after Zaria had a chance to nap, and drink a hot chocolate from a well-meaning Master Brown, stood blocking the entrance to the Thief of Peace's Passage. "This is just what we need."

"I sense a big fat 'NOT' in there," said Geirr, dryly.

"That's your cue to scram," added Christoffer helpfully.

Grimkell spread his hands wide. "Not happy to see me, I see. Don't worry, the feelings are mutual. It's time for you to leave and never return."

"You and what army?" challenged Aleks.

"Funny you should ask," Grimkell murmured as a sheet of fog descended and retracted, revealing Carita and Bendix. "There they are now. Let me properly introduce my associates. This is Carita, the true and proper ruler of the Winter Court, and Bendix, soon-to-be ruler of the Spring Court. We've come to ensure you get your wish. You don't have to be king of Niffleheim."

"How did you get around my father?" Saskia demanded, drawing her icicle blades.

"Fog," said Carita.

"Ensorcelled allies," said Bendix.

"Jelena and Rex," said Grimkell.

"They're not ensorcelled," said Bendix mildly. "They're with us because they want to be and because they don't want you alive."

Smug, Carita said, "You're not our king."

"No he is not," agreed Bendix.

The Spring fairy was a tall, slender man with soft brown hair and brown eyes. He could be anyone, but he exuded confidence and a certain *je ne sais quoi* that put you at ease without even speaking. Aleks blinked and forced himself to concentrate on something else. His mind drifted back to analyzing the new fey, and he had to wrench his gaze to Grimkell's. It took a lot of effort. Too much.

"The general has a lot on his hands right now," Grimkell said. "Let's get to business –"

"Abdicate the throne, or we'll be forced to kill you," Carita cut in. She was all honey and syrup, clearly relishing a chance to tear him down.

"I'm afraid you're behind the times," said Aleks, wondering if he should go for the bow across his back, or the sword at his hip. Maybe he wouldn't need either. "Zaria is back."

She stepped out and offered a little wave. "Hello, everyone. Let's be civil about this and nobody needs to be hurt."

Grimkell frowned. "Princess, stay out of this."

Nori strode between them. With an imperious little tilt of her head, she sneered down her nose. "Stand aside. You three are no match here. Not to the sorceress who defeated Koll."

"There's not to be a fight?" Zorka said, frowning and fingering the ends of her rainbow braid. "Less talk. More hitting. Please? I need blood. I need glory."

"If we must fight," said Bendix, in a bored tone. "Shall we begin?"

"Oh, you're on," agreed Zorka and charged, only to be flattened in an instance by gale-force winds.

Stronger than the winds used on the roof back in Summer, Aleks and the others were hurled back as if they were riding the Graviton at a carnival. They stuck on the walls at various heights, kept in place by the pressure. Not even Airi was spared. She squawked in panic. Aleks knew how she felt. One dip, a small fluctuation, and they'd be dropped like sacks of potatoes. It wouldn't be pleasant from this height.

Grimkell held out his hands, channeling his magic through them. "I'm running you out of Niffleheim once and for all," he said.

"You wish," snarled Aleks as he grabbed for the Trofast sword, but a simple hand motion from Grimkell batted it away. It clattered to the ground in a distant corner. He glowered impotently.

"I'm tired of waiting for you to fulfill your promise to me. If you won't leave on your own, I'll kill you here and now and claim the Fox Throne for myself."

"You'll have to get through me," Saskia screamed, the wind whipping her words away. The wind also whipped her blades away. They shattered against the ground.

"Coward," Nori said bitterly.

"That's rich," scoffed Grimkell. "Of all my children, you're the biggest disappointment."

"Funny," said Nori with dignity. "That's what I always said to others about you."

She choked and plummeted as Grimkell clenched his fist and sucked the air back to him as fast as he'd propelled it earlier. She landed hard against the ground, collapsing under the impact.

Zaria conjured a fireball, holding it in her fist. "My magic isn't physical. You're not going to knock my missile off course."

Grimkell's eyes widened, but he maintained his winds. She let loose and it sailed through them as if the air was still, and landed square in his chest, throwing him backwards into the passage's door, slamming it closed. He slumped to the ground dazed. The winds died instantly, and they fell.

"Ahh!" screamed Geirr, landing with a thud.

"A-are y-you oh-kay?" wheezed Nori, sucking down great gulps of air.

"I sh-should ah-ask you th-that," said Geirr, rolling over. "May-maybe I will wh-when I regain my br-breath."

Filip reached out to Zaria's prone form. "Zar-Zar, are you okay?" She didn't answer, which caused him to panic. He shook her. "Wake up, Zar-Zar. Wake up."

She groaned, and everyone breathed a sigh of relief. Aleks couldn't imagine facing what would come next without her. Her purple eyes opened, and she twisted around, pushing slowly to her feet. She wobbled, and Filip held her steady.

"Can't keep a good troll down," huffed Zorka, heaving upwards onto her feet. "Prepare for the feeling of my fists to your face. It's going to hurt."

"Stop," commanded Bendix, throwing out his hand.

Zorka did, her eyes glazing over. Bendix smirked, but his grin fell away when the mountain-troll shook her head and threw off his order, advancing slowly, like she was pushing against an irresistible force.

"Stop," he commanded again.

For a minute it looked like Zorka would pause again, but she resisted. Pushing into a bank of fog, she grabbed Carita in one hand and Bendix in the other, clunking their heads together and knocking them out. Tossing their limp bodies aside, she dusted her hands and said with smug superiority, "Magic powers are no match for the strength of a troll."

"Amen," said Christoffer. "Let's tie them up."

"I wonder why they didn't bring banner men?" asked Saskia. "Did they think we'd be pushovers?"

"Probably needed all of them to stay and fight Sivert," said Christoffer. "They assumed the three of them were powerful enough to take us out."

"That sounds about right to me," said Nori. "They figured we were bluffing about Zaria's presence down here, too. She took them by surprise."

"Zorka took them by surprise," Zaria protested weakly, leaning against Filip.

"Save your strength," he murmured, chaffing her arm. "You'll be needing it."

With the three fairies secured like prized Christmas hams, Aleks and Henrik heaved on the door closing off the passage and pulled it open. It groaned and shivered on its hinges, protesting every movement. Christoffer clapped his hands over his ears, grimacing. It was worse than the sound of fingernails on a chalkboard!

Alex peered into the space behind the door, expecting to see twin glowing eyes; but the darkened passage revealed nothing. Christoffer lowered his hands and scanned the area around him. "I don't like this," he said.

"We can't stop here. We have to keep going," said Henrik.

Geirr handed out flashlights to everyone. They traveled down the dusty, mirror-lined hall in pairs. Filip stuck close to Zaria. Aleks and Saskia trailed behind, with Geirr and Christoffer behind them, followed by Henrik and Nori, and finally Zorka who brought up the rear. Their reflections warped and wrinkled around them like so many shifting shadows waiting to jump-scare them. Aleks had felt more secure when, years ago, the mirrors had been covered with a thick layer of dust. This was too creepy.

Halfway to Jerndor, Zaria and Filip stumbled to a stop. Aleks was about to ask why, when he saw it. Mouth agape, he looked behind him at his sister. White rimmed her pupils, as fear gripped her. He spun back around.

Wedged in the bowing surface of a mirror like Winnie the Pooh in a tree, was the dragon they'd been looking for – snub snout, yellow eyes, pewter scales, and all. He stopped trying to push himself out and snapped his gaze toward them.

"You're too late, Princess," he crowed. "I'm free. At long last, I'm free."

"Not yet, you aren't," she taunted, a purple fireball bigger than any others that had come before flickered between her hands. "I'm going to send you right back where you belong."

Filip drew his short blade, exclaiming, "This is great! He can't defend himself."

A red hot fireball blasted down the passage.

"Watch out!" cried Zaria, the purple flame winking out as she pulled her boyfriend out from harm's way.

The blond teen yelped as the fire singed him, leaving a trail of heat, scorched hair, and smarted skin in its wake. Fritjof chuckled sinisterly.

"Yikes!" Filip echoed, licking his fingers and dabbing the still smoking remains, putting out the fire in his eyebrows.

Henrik drew his cloak closer. "Dragons breathe fire. We have to be careful."

"No kidding," said Filip, just shy of sarcasm. "So how do we do this?"

"Let's all attack him at once," suggested Saskia. "He can't shoot fireballs at all of us."

"I don't like this plan," Geirr complained, but he drew his sword. "Someone's going to get a fireball to the face."

"Charge!" cried Christoffer; racing past them, waving a dagger in the air.

They attacked. Knives slashed, daggers flew, swords struck, and magic blasted. In response, a massive fireball zinged at them, forcing them to dive out of the way. Zaria hurled another ball of purple magic, but it splashed harmlessly against the dragon's scaly armor.

299

"I'm stronger than my brothers," gloated Fritjof.

"Yeah, so?" sniffed Nori. "Even my strong, tough brother cries uncle, when I do this –"

She rammed her dagger up Fritjof's nose. He howled in pain, seizing back… and back… and back…

"ACHOO!"

The force of the sneeze shot Fritjof back through the mirror toward the Under Realm and Nori against the mirrors on the opposite wall in the passage. They splintered around her like a demented halo. She hung there in suspended animation, before falling like a ragdoll. The mirror Fritjof had gone through wobbled like loose-set jello.

"Nori!" cried Geirr.

Aleks ran and fell down beside her, hauling her into his arms tapping her face. "Nori. Nori! Wake up."

"She's unconscious," said Saskia, resting her fingers beneath the redhead's nose. "She's breathing. Leave her here. She'll be okay until we come back."

Reluctantly, he put his sister down, taking a moment to shift her to a more comfortable position. Snatching his bow off his back, he stood, clenching it tight.

"Me first," cawed Airi, shooting through the wonky mirror.

One-by-one they passed through to the other side. Aleks expected to feel as if he was moving through pudding, but the sensation, was like something else altogether. Instead of leaving them dry on the other side, the mirror spat them out like a toilet flushing, depositing them twenty feet above a thicket of trees beside the Gjöll River.

Aleks descended, along with the watery discharge, toward the knife-filled river below. Light glinted off their sleek, sharp edges, making them look like a swarm of piranhas. His panic broke when a golden tree limb snatched him from the sky and put him on the ground.

Zaria squelched down beside him a moment later. "That was different," she said, running her hands over her body sluicing the silver-gray gel-like substance off in chunks. "Gross."

Aleks looked up to see Henrik come through. On this side, the mirror-tunnel appeared to be a distorted silvery bubble, unformed and unnatural that dripped liquid metal raindrops. They fell into the Gjöll with a hiss, sending steam up and over the waves. Aleks watched the knives flash toward the mirror-drops like a shiver of sharks in the midst of a feeding frenzy.

"I don't know how to close that hole," said Zaria, watching it with concern. "That's a rip in the void.

Fritjof's completely bypassed the barrier the Golden Kings provide."

"We can figure that out after stopping him."

Christoffer and Filip landed in the river, but the knives ignored them. They were human and utterly devoid of magic, which made them harmless. If any others in their party, save Geirr, had landed in the river the knives would have been on them in a heartbeat, slicing and cutting into them, draining their magic and their lives in one fell swoop.

Henrik and Saskia lent hands to haul the two dripping teens out of the water. The river, which ran serpentine-like through the Under Realm, guarded the real world from its dragon prisoners. Flying over it was out of the question because of the fairies' void and the ellefolken kings' barrier, and Fritjof wouldn't dare cross it for fear of losing his powers.

The forest seemed eerily calm and quiet. He whipped his head around searching for danger.

"I don't like this," said Geirr beside him.

Zorka retied her ears and asked the question they all were thinking, "Where's Fritjof?"

Filip gripped his short sword tighter. "Isn't he too big to hide?"

At the mention of Koll's youngest brother, a windy whistling sort of noise blew past Aleks. He spun around, only to be knocked a dozen feet into the air. Zaria crashed into him, and they fell against an alder tree, splintering it. The cry it gave caused his heart to clench in pain and fear. That had been one of the ellefolken women.

"You foolish children," hissed Fritjof as they scrambled to their feet.

"Where is he?" Zaria whispered.

Aleks notched his arrow and sighted down his arm. He searched for the dragon, following the low menacing voice. There! Too fast to follow, its great bloated body slithered between the trees.

"I am the dragon to cut whole armies down, I made leaders of men wet themselves at the very sight of me, and you think the seven of you will STOP ME?"

He had a point. Hadn't Grimkell, Carita, and Bendix proved that just a short time ago? What could Aleks and the others possibly do that an army couldn't do better? Hadn't he wanted Sivert's soldiers and the rest of Niffleheim to come together for this very purpose? What was he thinking being down here without the numbers?

Fritjof reared up and knocked several trees aside, toppling them to the ground like a child knocking over a bouquet of pencils. Aleks grimaced as their cries died, loosing his arrow. Zaria beside him did the same with her fireball. The twin attacks barreled down on the dragon. He batted them aside with his twin tails.

His yellow eyes narrowed. "I'm insulted."

His tails snaked out and snatched up Christoffer and Filip from their encroaching position as if he had eyes in the back of his head. Fritjof knocked them together, their skulls cracking like acorns smacking into glass, and flung them aside, just as Zorka had done recently with Carita and Bendix.

"NO!" shouted Zaria, desperate to save them.

In an instant she'd left his side and caught them on conjured mattresses. The effort staggered her, and she collapsed on top of Filip. Nonplussed, Fritjof reared back, hissing.

"You have thought magic," he accused. "That's why Koll wanted you under his spell and didn't kill you as was the plan. I won't make the same mistake, Princess."

"Zaria!" Henrik cried out in warning, but it was too late.

A giant specimen of a tree crashed onto her back, pinning her and Filip to the mattress. Zorka and

Henrik raced over, but the Stag Lord got there first, dropped his sword and lifted the tree, allowing Filip to pull himself and Zaria out from under. All those days the Stag Lord spent moving rocks for the witch of the woods paid off in that moment. Had she known Henrik would need that kind of strength?

Zorka reached them then and helped him to gently set it aside. Henrik paused grimly beside his fallen subject, resting a silent hand against the trunk in sorrow and regret. The troll handed him back his sword and he took it standing up, turning to face the battle, his gaze flickering over the sorceress, checking on her health.

Filip brushed Zaria's hair back from her face, but despite his tender ministrations she remained unconscious. Aleks gulped. They needed her special powers. Where was her mother, the queen, when you needed backup? He looked up almost expecting to see her soar to their rescue. They were going to need rescuing. This confrontation had been stupid.

Placing Zaria down softly, Filip snatched the Drakeland Sword from her side and surged to his feet. Henrik tried to stop him, but the teen swerved and charged one of Fritjof's tails. The dragon flicked him away like a horse shooing away a pesky fly. He crumpled to the ground, following Zaria's fate, and the sword flew off into the distance.

"I think we're going to need this," said Geirr, handing Aleks a small object.

He opened his palm and saw a single golden coin with an embossed floral motif. Shocked, he met his friend's level gaze.

"Where? When?"

But those were pointless questions because he knew where and when. Hadn't he found a coin in the corridor by the well earlier, too?

He clapped his friend's shoulder. "You saved us, Geirr. This is exactly what we need." Raising it above his head, he shouted, "I wish Fritjof dead!"

The coin disappeared, but Fritjof, having paused in his pursuit merely smirked, his tongue darting out to wet his lipless snout.

"Did you think the power of the well enough to stop me? Fool."

He had, actually. The fact that it hadn't worked left him feeling adrift at sea. He could only watch as Saskia and Henrik tag-teamed one tail while Zorka attempted to wrestle the other one.

While Zorka was whipped around like a cowboy on a bucking bronco, Saskia flung wave after wave of icicles. Henrik swung his great sword with all his strength, but the sword kept bucking away from the fight, jerking itself out of Henrik's hands, as if scared. He lunged for it, ducking under a swipe from Fritjof's other tail. It skittered away, as if possessed.

"We need the Drakeland Sword!" shouted Christoffer, dodging Fritjof's tails and fiery breath.

He and Geirr circled Fritjof, jumping and crashing into each other to avoid the dragon's dual counter attacks. Geirr slipped once on the muddy river bank, and it was enough. Fritjof hurtled him hundreds of feet in the air. Aleks knew just what this sort of event would do to Geirr's fear of heights and cringed. Airi tried to offer assistance, but had to dodge Fritjof's snapping teeth and blazing fire.

"Grab him!" he shouted desperately to the alder trees surrounding them.

They heeded him not. Catching Henrik's attention Aleks pleaded with his eyes. The Stag Lord touched the trunk of a tree next to him and closed his eyes. The alder shuddered and swayed. Branches moved and rustled, linking with their neighbors and their limbs shot forward to battle the dragon as he played with his newfound toy like a cat with catnip.

Screaming in fright from another toss, Geirr covered his face. Fritjof fought the trees, breaking their grasping limbs at the roots, and Aleks gasped in horror as the dragon deliberately let his friend crash into the ground. Geirr didn't move. Three of his friends were down for the count. 'They should have waited,' became a constant refrain in his head.

Aleks loosed arrow after arrow, but they sailed harmlessly by, missing their intended target by miles. Furious, he redoubled his efforts, but no matter how fast he shot, Fritjof took out his friends one by one by one. A blast of fire melted Saskia's wave of ice and sent her to the ground. Henrik was bashed against his brethren, and the ellefolken wept at his downfall. Aleks fought back panic.

His vision tunneled, and all he could think of to do was to provide cover for Christoffer as he wended his way over branch and tail, dodging fire and insults. With a cry of triumph the spiky-haired teen flung himself forward, snatching up the Drakeland Sword. It answered the call, whizzing around to fight Fritjof, as if it had a mind of its own, but even its powers failed to protect him from the dragon of chaos. When Christoffer's fancy footwork faltered, a tail clotheslined him, knocking him out, pinning the sword underneath him.

Zorka lasted longer, being more impervious to physical and magical attacks. She picked up the Drakeland Sword and turned to fight, but she herself had never wielded any weapon other than her fists, so she and the sword attacked, at odds with each other. The sword tried to compensate and so did she, but

Fritjof just hit back harder, until she too, fell like a sack of potatoes, shaking the earth.

Aleks' stomach sank. In minutes Fritjof had wiped out all of them. He'd warned them that seven wouldn't be enough to do the job. What was there left to do now? What hope did he have alone? He felt sick. As if in a trance, he began to lower his bow.

Airi sent out a sharp ca-caw. "Snap out! Snap out!"

Her cry penetrated the deep fog that encased his senses. Aleks looked up and spied her dive bombing the dragon. Fritjof sent out a blast of fire, forcing Airi to change direction. She sailed away, shrieking in fright as the heat singed her tail feathers. Aleks lifted his bow and shot an arrow at Fritjof.

It bounced harmlessly off the dragon's scales, but it drew his attention. The bow was knocked from his hands as the dragon's tail grabbed him by an ankle and drew him high in the air. Flailing upside down, Aleks felt an extraordinary sense of déjà vu, as if he'd been in this predicament before.

Fritjof played with him, flinging him down toward the ground. He yelled, the air ripping from his lungs as he plummeted, only to be snapped back into the air. Up and down he went like a yo-yo to the amusement of Fritjof, who roared with pleasure. Airi tried to help, but the dragon kept her at bay with his flame and second tail.

The smell of electricity crackled in the air, gathering in tight little coils, ready to spring. The hair on the back of his neck rose, and his arms broke out into gooseflesh. The air pressed thickly against him, heavy and unbreathable. Aleks struggled to maintain his orientation and the contents of his stomach.

Airi cried out again, her sharp piercing calls keeping Aleks focused despite the turbulence that swirled through his senses. He couldn't be lost in the storm with Airi by his side. She'd protect him from Fritjof.

The oppressive dullness in the atmosphere coiled tighter and tighter, until at last the clouds of chaos unleashed their fury. Rain began to pelt down, cloaking the scene. In seconds, Aleks was soaked through, his hair plastered to his skull and his clothes to his body. It dripped into his eyes, making it hard to see, and he fought to clear them.

"Give up, Changeling," Fritjof snarled, drawing him closer. "Stop fighting me. It's over."

"Never," Aleks cried out, finding he had some bit of hope in him that things might turn around for the better. Zaria might wake up. Queen Helena might arrive. He yelped as the dragon dropped him again.

Aleks must have spoken aloud for Fritjof hissed, "Queen Helena is not coming. I took care of her."

"Just like you took care of Zaria?" Aleks asked.

"I could be your best friend, if only you would let me," Fritjof said, changing course.

"Ha!" scoffed Aleks.

Fritjof growled, spinning Aleks around and bringing him closer so that they were eye level with each other. Aleks stared in dread at the yellow eye the size of a dinner plate. Sweat and rain trickled down his back, indistinguishable from each other.

The dragon pressed his fangs against Aleks' skin. "We could do great things together. We could overhaul the fairies' government. We could rejoin the world with our powers fully intact. We could make it better, you and I. I'm the best friend you'll ever have. What do you say?"

"I have friends. I don't need you," Aleks said, disgusted by the feel of Fritjof pressed against him. It felt like he imagined being hugged by his aunt would feel like, oddly firm and squishy.

The yellow eye narrowed into a slit. "You don't know what you need. You're lost. You're alone. You're trapped. You have no weapons that can stand against me. There's nobody to help you and there's nothing you can do to help them."

Aleks looked down below and stared at the prone forms of his friends. It was true that he couldn't help them, or they he. It was probably true, too, that he couldn't help himself. His prospects were dire. Hopelessness encased him like a blanket, threatening to overwhelm him.

Airi cawed, "Me! You have me!"

She swooped down and pecked at Fritjof's eyes. He snarled and snapped, catching some of her white feathers in his teeth, pulling them out. She faltered in her flight, spiraling out of control.

"Watch out," Aleks shouted, but it was too late.

Airi struggled in the storm, flying haphazardly. Fritjof swiped at her and sent the raven flying into the roots of the ellefolken. Her frightened squawk cut short.

"No!" Aleks cried, struggling against Fritjof's hold.

The white raven tumbled down in a freefall. The nearby ellefolken used their tree roots to bring her safely to the ground. Aleks couldn't bear to watch. His heart broke, and he feared the worst. She was so much smaller than the others.

Airi was his to protect. She was his friend, and he hers. They had to stick together. He couldn't lose her.

He couldn't bear to think of not hearing her taunt him, or nip at his ear, or cuff him with her feathers, or –

Fritjof hooted triumphantly, and Aleks knew he was lost. He blinked back tears. Everything that the dragon had said had come true. He was alone. He was friendless. He was trapped and unarmed. It was hopeless… useless. He was useless.

The dragon, sensing that Aleks' resolve had faltered, dropped him. Aleks' stomach swooped and rolled once again, as he was jerked around like a mouse being played with by a tiger. Catching him by the foot, Fritjof dangled him upside down. A claw prodded his stomach.

"Say you give up, Changeling, and this can all be over," Fritjof cajoled.

Aleks stubbornly shook his head. He would never give in. Fritjof would have to kill him. For Airi. For Saskia and his friends. For the world. While there was anything left in him to give, he would give it, anything except capitulation to the very creature that stole everything from him.

"You're weak!" shouted Fritjof. "You can't save anybody. It's far, far, too late."

The louder Fritjof roared, trying to convince him to give up and give in, the more Aleks drowned him out.

A mighty wind could howl only so long before its roar faded into white noise. The more Fritjof tried to create a tempest in Aleks, the quieter he became.

Lies. It was all lies. Aleks felt the truth deep within take root, as if he suddenly had Nori's keen sense of it. He knew what to do, because he knew who he was. He was changeling, he was fey, he was human. He was the best of each. No matter what Fritjof claimed, he could not take away Aleks' identity or purpose. It could not be shaken loose. It was who he was, who he always would be.

He stared the dragon down, ignoring all the discomforts of his position, totally calm. He saw the instant Fritjof realized he'd lost. Those huge yellow eyes widened in fear. The dragon screamed, his foul heated breath blazing across Aleks' face like a blast from a volcano. He didn't flinch when sharp teeth gnashed before his nose. Fritjof squeezed him tighter with his tails, but Aleks barely felt it under the wave of peace that rolled over him.

Truth does not need to know its opposite in order to know it is true. By its very nature it is truth, and the lie isn't required to legitimize it. Aleks didn't need Fritjof around to give him purpose, or a reason to be himself. Fritjof was the lie and therefore unnecessary and unreal. Aleks knew his place and would never be lost again. The chaos within was tamed, and in its place all was harmony.

Fritjof shrieked as if burnt, dropping Aleks. Plummeting, he landed with a hard thud on the ground next to Zorka and the Drakeland Sword. Grasping it, Aleks carefully pried it loose and stood, shaking his wet bangs out of his eyes.

Fritjof curled protectively around his tail, which looked blackened with what appeared to be scorch marks. Licking it like a wounded animal, he spat, "How did you do this?"

Aleks brought the sword in front of him. "I'll give you the same courtesy you gave me. You've lost. Give up now and surrender."

"You'd like that, wouldn't you?" Fritjof gnashed, lashing out with his tails, coming at Aleks from two opposite directions.

Aleks slashed at one, the sword making it easy, as it leapt forward eagerly in his hands. The indomitable sword would never give up, and neither would he. Spinning fast, he swiped at the other tail. The sword nearly jerked itself out of his hands as it spun around and struck, lodging in the first tail. Fritjof howled, yanking his tail backwards, taking the sword with it.

He scrambled away, climbing over and under alder roots, searching for his bow. He was an archer, not a swordsman. The twin tails slapped down on the ground around him, forcing Aleks to duck and roll to avoid being turned into a pancake.

At the next pass, he twisted and instead of grasping his bow, found the sword, but Fritjof sensing the desperate attempt to gain control of the Drakeland Sword, grabbed for it, too. At the dragon's foul touch, and under its tight claws, the sword cracked.

"What? No! That's not supposed to happen," shouted Aleks, but it was too late; light shone from the cracks and the Drakeland Sword splintered much like the alder tree before it, and the mirrors before that. It would never be whole again. The pieces showered down, and disappeared with the rain.

Cackling, Fritjof threw Aleks aside and lunged for the nearby bow. Too numb to think, Aleks didn't move fast enough. The dragon swooped in and clutched it between his talons before flying off with it. He tossed it into the Gjöll and roared with satisfaction.

Aleks watched mutely, his brow pulled into a heavy crease, as his last chance to stop Fritjof disappeared below the river's glittering and roiling surface. What could he do now? The Drakeland Sword was gone, broken, and his bow hidden in the waters of a magic river that would kill him if he stepped foot in it.

Fritjof must have thought the same thing because his lipless mouth pulled back in a vile smirk. "I got you now, Changeling. You're dead."

The dragon transformed, his visage melting into his true form. Like wind, he became invisible, terrifying Aleks who thought things couldn't get any worse. This dragon had the combined powers of Grimkell and Eskil, his cousin.

"What next?" he wondered, looking skyward for an answer.

Lightning crackled and rain blew harder. The first blow knocked him backward twenty feet. The second threw him down closer to the frothing river. Rain barreled down in relentless sheets, but as Aleks peered into the gloom, he realized something. Excitement bubbled up as the realization dawned.

The force of Fritjof's movements revealed his location, just as leaves did when the wind danced through them. If Aleks' paid attention he could see the rain pelt Fritjof's invisible form and slide off. An idea came to Aleks, and he knew he'd only have one shot at it.

Picking himself up, he ran toward the river, willing to lose his magic in order to save his friends. His hair lifted as the dragon whirled around him, tearing at his clothes. Fritjof pushed him toward the river in large irrepressible gusts, not realizing that was exactly where Aleks wished to go.

"Do you know what the Gjöll does to magic beings that fall within it?" Fritjof taunted, swirling around Aleks and pushing him along.

Of course he knew, that's why Aleks scrambled for purchase, to delay the dip into the Gjöll, until he was right on top of where the bow had disappeared. He stumbled into the water, and immediately felt its repulsion, as it tried to blast him backwards.

But the river couldn't fight the oppressive force of Fritjof's winds, which pushed and dragged Aleks deeper into the river. Rain dripped steadily into his eyes, obscuring his vision. He had to get his bow. There was no time to lose.

The knives and daggers flashed, turning and swarming toward him. Just as he was wondering if this was a foolish venture, Aleks spied the bow beneath the churning surface as a bolt of lightning lit the sky. He dove and grabbed it as the first knives reached him, slashing at his skin.

The pain was unimaginable as the knives drew his magic from him. He bit his lip hard to avoid crying out. He couldn't give up now, even as his body begged him to stop, to escape. In the swirling mass of silver, Aleks spotted what he was searching for and plucked it from the water. A stiletto dagger wriggled and bucked, fighting him hard, and slicing his palm.

"Don't fight me," he told it, wincing as it got him again. "I need your help to stop a dragon."

Understanding, it stopped fighting, going limp in his hand. Letting go a sigh of relief, Aleks lined it up with the bow and prayed that what he was about to do would work. He positioned his bow and aimed for the heart of the swirling vortex that was Fritjof. Using the rain and wind to guide his aim, Aleks held, watching and waiting for a true strike.

He ignored the bites of blades sinking into his legs and the exhaustion that pulled at him. Trembling and shaking all over, Aleks fought to keep his aim true. Water dripped into his eyes, forcing him to blink rapidly to clear his vision. One shot. He needed one clear shot.

The feel of his magic draining away staggered him. Its loss a debilitating blow he hadn't expected, but there was no other way. He knew in mere moments it would be gone. The sense that what he was about to do was the right thing left him. Aleks ignored the sudden influx of panic and turmoil.

His magic, which had always guided him, was the price for one less dragon in the world. As it left him, his vision blurred, and he swayed on his feet.

Concentrating, Aleks used its remaining vestiges to make his target true.

In that moment of composure, when all seemed silent and calm, Aleks adjusted his aim once more. With conviction he let it fly. The dagger sung in the air, wobbling in its course.

He held his breath, waiting, watching, hoping for a direct hit. The dagger sluiced through the eye of the storm and Aleks laughed, falling to his knees in the water. He'd done it. He'd hit the dragon's heart.

Fritjof howled, and it was a death knell pealing over the Under Realm. The winds died in their tracks, the lightning cracked and faded with a whimper, the rains quit, and the ugly awful uncertainty that had plagued him shattered, leaving only peace. The light from the Golden Kings broke apart the gloom, and a rainbow of colors splashed against the roots of the alder trees, filtering through to linger and bless all it touched.

When a shaft of light hit him, Aleks felt relief. He had done it. He had defeated the Thief of Peace. Aleks' vision spun, and he was brought back to himself as the knives flashed past him. With desperate movements, he dragged himself towards the river's bank, not wanting to drown when he passed out.

Stained red with his blood the Gjöll no longer fought him, knowing he had made his way back to the side of the Under Realm, to the prison it was meant to guard. Knowing too, he had nothing left to give. His arms and legs felt like lead. He could barely move. The current flowed around him, sending him forward. The knives and daggers flitted away, leaving him in peace, having completed their deadly purpose. His magic was gone.

Aleks waded, stumbling onto the shoreline. He didn't dare look down at his legs, not wanting to see how deep the Gjöll had cut him. As he lost sight of the world, slipping into sleep, he smiled hearing his friends as they awoke from Fritjof's spell. He even heard a faint ca-caw and knew all would be right again. All he wanted now was to sleep.

***

She woke him with a kiss. Aleks opened his eyes to see an angelic face watching him with concern emanating from her sapphire eyes. He sighed happily.

"I must be in heaven."

"I beg your pardon?" she asked, confused.

"You're an angel."

Out of sight, Christoffer busted out laughing. "Oh man, you're such a sap. That's like the worst pick-up line ever. Seriously, you should let me give you pointers."

His face heated uncomfortably at being caught, and shaking the remnants of sleep from his brain, he sat up. Grabbing a pillow and chucking it at his friend, he growled, "Shut up, Christoffer."

Saskia tenderly brushed hair away from his forehead, her hand cool against his brow. "You had us all worried," she said.

"What happened?" he asked, propping himself up with a groan. His legs felt on fire.

"Easy, Red," she said, helping him up and after taking back the pillow projectile, fluffing his pillows. "Airi reached you first. She landed by your head and listened to see if you were breathing."

"Pecked you on the forehead, too," added Christoffer. "Left you a great big goose egg."

"It's almost gone," Saskia assured him when he tried to search for it. "When you didn't wake, she attacked your cuff."

Aleks lifted his wrist. The cuff looked like someone had hit it with a hammer, warping its smooth raven visage, and causing the leather on either side to fray. "Why was she going after this? It's my connection to the Lost Well."

"Airi can tell you for herself," said Saskia, calling the raven over. "She's a very smart girl. She knew exactly what to do to save you."

The white bird landed on her shoulder, cooing like a freaking dove, and nuzzled her hand as Saskia stroked her breast. She even raised a wing to protect Saskia as she continued petting. Aleks felt his heart clench. What wouldn't he do for the two females before him? They were part of him – the best part. Let Christoffer call him a sap.

"Go on Airi, tell him what you did," she murmured.

His raven flew-hopped to his lap, where his hands rested against his thighs. She tapped the cuff, cawing, "Cuff on. Aleks stay. Cuff off. Well take Aleks."

Aleks met Saskia's eyes in understanding. He'd been asleep so with the cuff gone he would've woken up in the well. He brushed his knuckles against the soft downy white feathers at the back of Airi's head. "You undid the latch," he guessed.

Airi nodded, puffing out her chest. "Well take Aleks. Aleks get better. Get better."

He picked her up and placed a kiss on her crown, before transferring her to his shoulder. "I got better," he agreed. "You did good, girl."

"The Lost Well's magic saved you," said Christoffer, coming over and sitting on the edge of the bed. "When it first took you, we all panicked."

"But Zaria figured it out," Saskia said, "She recognized the red flames."

"We all ran back to get you with Saskia leading the way. Man, can she run," said Christoffer. "I should probably go wake the others. It took Nori threatening them with a recitation of a poem she wrote about the dumb things humans do, to get them to sleep. Geirr actually said he'd listen, but she ran him off anyway."

"Then how come you're here?" asked Aleks, hiding a yawn behind his hand. "Shouldn't you both be asleep too? Not that I mind. I'm glad you're here."

"Couldn't sleep," said Christoffer. "Had to know you were all right. Plus I got a funny feeling about how the whole thing went down."

Saskia sensed the question in his gaze and clarified, "He thinks the mirror to the passage may have been used."

"I saw something," he said, frowning. "At least I think I did. Hard to be certain in all that rain."

Saskia rolled her eyes. "Nobody else saw anything," she said, soothing his bed covers. "In the Under Realm or in the passage. A dragon is too big to hide."

"What?" asked Aleks, confused. He thought he'd taken care of Fritjof.

"He's concerned another dragon escaped," she explained.

"He has a right to be," said a new voice, breezing into the room carrying a bowl of steaming liquid.

Aleks recognized the voice as belonging to the witch of the woods. "What are you doing here?" he asked.

"Welcoming Niffleheim back to the world," the witch said airily, before adding archly, "Perhaps this time they won't screw things up."

His eyebrows knit together. "What do you mean welcoming back to the world?"

"The Lost Well is now visible, both day and night, from above and below, all day, every day."

Aleks' eyes widened. "When did that happen?"

"When you destroyed Fritjof. The curse hiding the well from the fey lifted as per the Dragomir Treaty. Without him around to steal its power or to influence the fey toward evil, it is no longer necessary to hide it from them."

"But what about the other dragons?"

"None could permeate the court or meddle with it quite like the dragon of chaos. His special brand of mayhem suited the fey, and fed off their constant power-hungry attempts to control the realm."

He nodded slowly. At least something in this mess had a positive outcome; too bad he wouldn't be able to enjoy it. "How did you know I would become king?" he asked, remembering her prediction. "Was it prophecy?"

"Hardly," she scoffed. "It was a simple matter of deduction."

"Deduction?" Christoffer asked, incredulously. "How do you deduce something like that? He's always wanted to be human."

"Hmm…" said the witch noncommittally. "Your friend's gift is unique. The ability to navigate."

"So?" Aleks and Christoffer asked at the same time.

"That's a talent that can't be banished, hidden, diminished, ignored, forgotten, or lost. No matter how hard one would wish it."

Now Saskia looked confused. "I don't understand. The rules of the fey, of changelings – it shouldn't be possible."

"But it is," said the witch.

"The Lost Well turned me back into a fully-fledged fey?" asked Aleks.

"Yes, and no; it accelerated the process. Remember, I said you could spend time with me and get your powers back, too."

"Then I was always destined to be king? Not that I lasted very long."

It was a kingship he couldn't have anymore, not without powers. Saskia squeezed his hand, and Aleks felt bereft. He was going to lose her. She wouldn't want him without his magic gifts.

The witch, when she answered, said mysteriously, "In spite of everyone and everything trying to stand in your way, including yourself, you were always going to find what you needed for happiness."

"And that was a kingship?"

"Perhaps, but I think you and I know it was something else." The witch flicked her gaze to Saskia.

"Or someone else," Christoffer said, waggling his eyebrows. "Lover-boy here couldn't be without his Ice Queen."

The witch showed off her snaggletooth. "Your compass will always point you to the north star of your being. If you trust in it, you will always be guided rightly."

Aleks pondered this, thinking that didn't sound too bad. He sighed, "I don't have powers anymore. The Gjöll – the knives – my legs –"

Airi nibbled on his ear. "Well save Aleks. Powers return."

"Doesn't feel like they did," he said, focusing inward.

"There's a spark," said the witch. "It's up to you to nurse it now. The choice is yours to make. Are you a king? Are you fey? Are you human?"

Nori slammed into the room and cried, "You're awake!" She scooped him into a hug, her flaming red hair blocking his vision.

"I was already crowned," said Aleks, frowning at the witch, patting Nori's head awkwardly. "I don't have a choice. If I have my powers, then I'm still king."

Nori pulled back. "The coronation was botched and we didn't finish saying everything that needed to be said in the ceremony. You have a choice."

He looked between her and the others, something like happiness bubbling up in him. Grasping Saskia's hand he said, simply, warmly, "There's no choice to make."

"Good," said Nori. "Then we'll set up the whole thing again. Nobody will dare to stand against you, not now, after you destroyed a dragon. With Fritjof gone, everyone remembers him and how it was before. They've put two and two together and made four. Finally. You saved us. You saved us all."

With her words, Aleks concentrated and found he had the missing pieces to his memory. He could recall how the fighting originally took place in the Under Realm. He remembered going against Egil and Fritjof. It was no wonder he had had that case of déjà vu earlier.

"They'll be more impressed that he beat Grimkell, Carita, and Bendix," predicted Saskia.

Bemused, Aleks asked, "Will they really?"

She nodded, brushing his hair aside. "I'm glad you're staying, Red. Niffleheim needs you. I need you."

"Get a room," Christoffer joked, but Nori hushed him.

"I can't stay forever," said Aleks. "I have to go home to my parents. I have to finish school."

"In due time," said the witch, tending to him. "Let the well do its work. Let it heal you. Let it restore your magic."

"Saskia and I will plan for another coronation," Nori added.

"I will?" she asked, teasingly.

"You will," Nori stated imperiously. "Now I'm thinking bigger – more spectacular. We'll employ the most skilled fey to do what they do best. It'll be a coronation to remember, even in direct comparison to the aborted one from today. Young fairies will sigh over it for a lifetime."

As Nori droned on, Saskia looked at Aleks, and swept him up in her gaze once more. "Stay?" she asked.

"Yes," he said, feeling at peace.

Epilogue: If the Crown Fits

Early on Aleks met with Sivert, and the general, having his thumb on the pulse of Niffleheim, deemed it safe enough for him to wander around so long as someone was with him – even if that someone was one of his human friends. Grimkell, Carita, and Bendix were put in the dungeons, along with Jelena and Rex, where they awaited their trials. Nori told him he might have to use the well to strip them of their powers. It would be hard for him to do, but if their peers felt it just, he would make those wishes.

Aleks sent Airi out to the dwarves a second time. This time her message made it through and King Flein contacted him on the third day. The war between the two realms ended immediately. Aleks exchanged his prisoners, including Floki, in return for a future boon from the dwarf king.

Aleks didn't think the prince would come to a good end this time, not after seeing how angry Flein had been. The Ravager captain's fate remained to be seen… she at least had seemed contrite. Her two soldiers and the other Ravagers would most likely be safe from court martial, merely following their superior's orders.

Days slipped by as Aleks recuperated. Every morning he woke in the Lost Well. He had Zaria conjure him a bed and a chair in there so he could be more comfortable. He'd gotten quite tired of gold coins poking him in the back. As she went about her quiet task, they spoke about the Drakeland Sword.

"I haven't told Helena it's broken," Zaria whispered, as if afraid a dragon would hear her.

Queen Helena had been found, wounded and weak with pain in the Under Realm. Under the tender mercies of some former Niffleheim brownies, the sorceress queen was recovering. There was so much to do to repair the rift between the realms.

"I had the chance when she consulted with the fey void master, but I just couldn't."

"Why not?" asked Aleks, feeling sympathetic to her plight. It would not be fun news to break.

Zaria shook her head. "Because she'll be devastated... and disappointed. It was the only sword in existence that could stand up to the dragons. Not even Henrik's great sword stood a chance against Fritjof. He told me how it behaved."

"We're going to need something," said Aleks. "We can't rely on a fish-knife to do the trick again."

She nodded, glumly. "Who knows if the dwarves would make another? Could we trust them to? They've been so easily swayed."

"Queen Helena could sort that out," Aleks said.

"Perhaps," Zaria murmured, feeling the burden of indecision.

She would have to confess the sword's state to her birth mother sooner or later. He didn't have to say that though, she already knew, if he judged the slump of her shoulders right. It wasn't like the sword's state was her fault anyway. It broke because of Fritjof.

"Could you do me one more favor?" he asked.

"Anything," she said.

"Can you ensure the well is hidden from those who wish to use its powers for ill? Do you have all your strength back? It wouldn't be too much, would it?"

"I'm back to normal," she said. "I can do this."

The spell she wove shone like lilacs in sunshine, and once more the Lost Well was protected against the fey whose greed would have them use it to harm others. Aleks breathed a sigh of relief, feeling that weight slip off his shoulders. Others would be able to find it, but he wouldn't go advertising that. Let the well draw to it those who were worthy.

He knew his friends were anxious to return home, to set the time stream back to rights, but nobody broached him with the topic. It took eight days before he could transform into a fox again. He'd missed his birthday, but he didn't care.

He and Saskia celebrated his change with a race across the plains. They gamboled and played, and she showed him the sights. Things he hadn't seen before.

In the Summer Court he found a surging waterfall, which poured from the icy ceiling in a turquoise plume. At Winter, she showed him her stomping grounds, which made him feel more connected to her than ever before. In Spring, they played tag in a field filled with small white flowers.

He spent much of his remaining time meeting with any fey who stopped to have a word with him and avoiding Nori as she planned his second coronation like an army sergeant. Even Sivert was impressed.

From his conversations he gleaned that many of the weaker fey were ready for change. It seemed like hope was bubbling in Niffleheim like yeast and soon the whole void would change. He had a few wishes in mind to try to accomplish that.

The first wish hid the secret passages within every court. They would only reveal themselves when an innocent's life was in danger. He didn't want to close them permanently, but he had to do something to create the culture shift he was seeking.

Geirr caught up with him on the day of his coronation. As Aleks readied himself, they talked about the future, something Aleks had been contemplating more and more. What did the days ahead hold for him? For his friends?

"Will you come home after this?"

Aleks shook his head. "Not yet, but soon. I have to get things settled here. I have plans to put into place. My sister and Saskia will have to be granted rights to make decisions and joint-rule in my absence."

Geirr nodded thoughtfully. "Have you thought about the laws you'll enact then?"

He grinned, ear-to-pointy-ear, eager to share his plans. "I'm going to rescind the laws on kits and changelings. Any fey family can have any number of children. Changelings won't be banished anymore by pain of death from Niffleheim, nor will they be marked."

"You'll enforce that they can't make changelings though, right?" Geirr asked, knowingly.

"Actually," said Aleks. "I'll only enforce that they can't turn human children into changelings and bring them to Niffleheim. I turned out all right, but I'm going to insist that they consult the witch of the woods for placement if they go that route."

"She'll love you for that," Geirr said wryly. "How much did that bit of negotiation cost you?"

"None," Aleks said smirking. "She doesn't know it yet. In fact, I don't plan to tell the meddling old witch anything about it. Let her find out later if the time ever comes."

"I'd pay to be in her clearing when that conversation takes place."

Aleks laughed. "Better you than me. After all that, I intend to collapse the court structure. No more of this us-versus-them mentality. I'm going to insist on more cities being built to help with that."

"You still have to make Sivert and his associates noble," Geirr pointed out.

"And I will," said Aleks. "I won't strip everything from the fey. I wish to preserve as much as I change."

"What about telling them that the Lost Well is permanently open?"

Aleks told him about what he'd asked Zaria to do. "I think instead I'll work with the master void designers to create openings to Norway. It's important that we're not isolated anymore."

The coronation that day was everything Nori planned for and more. Every fey, young and old, skilled or not, took their talents and wielded something for the event. Niffleheim fairly glowed like a miniature sun from all that magic.

Saskia stood beside him, arrayed in cloth as soft and flowing as a gently falling snowflake. His friends cheered him from the crowd. He knew where he fit in this world, in this realm, and with the fey. They watched him with joyful expectation and anticipation of what his reign would bring. The crown, when it was fit to his brow, had never felt more right.

Afterwards, everybody celebrated including visiting dignitaries. Both King Flein and King Kafirr arrived through the Thief of Peace's Passage with their contingencies. Queen Helena appeared, escorting

Queen Silje, Olaf, and some elves and ellefolken. The witch of the woods immediately sought the queen sorceress out for a chat.

Aleks recognized many faces and waved in welcome. The field surrounding the Firething broke out into a party that rivaled the one at Koll's demise. Everyone was euphoric, and there wasn't a frown to mar the scene – except one. Kanutte was as jealous as Zorka had predicted and the teenage troll fumed on the sidelines, as all her friends swarmed the rainbow-haired troll to get the juicy details firsthand.

Granny from the Hidden Gem brought him a trinket but he had no idea what to do with it. It appeared to be a cheese slicer, but when she said, "It's only sliced off a finger or two in its day," he knew he wouldn't trust the magic enough to use it. Luckily, Airi was keen for it and took it away to her hidey hole.

Hillevi and Hertha appeared, unarmed and in civilian clothing. Their profuse thanks for saving them – and Saskia wrapping a possessive arm around his waist – had him blushing. Only when the winterling brought out her icicles did they depart.

As they slipped back into the reveling crowd, he spied Frigga in the midst of the dwarfish contingent. She appeared mulish, but subdued. A mug of cider dripped down her hand from where a jovial beardless dwarf had shoved it. She eyed it and the male in disgust, before she glanced at him, sensing his eyes on her. She raised the mug and chugged it, holding his gaze through it all before grimacing and backhanding her mouth.

The moment ended when another fairy came to congratulate him on his victory. Saskia had been right, more fey than not seemed overawed at his handling of the various court rulers of Niffleheim than the dragon. He shook his head in wonder at it. Perhaps it was because they'd been more visibly entrenched in their day to day than Fritjof.

As the evening wore on, Falkor sidled up beside Aleks, holding a mug of cider the size of a small barrel. Aleks clinked his much smaller mug against the troll's in greeting. "Your mission was successful, I see," he said, watching King Kaffir dance with a laughing Zaria.

Falkor glared at him balefully, "Yes, but you have put me in the worst position possible. You're no friend."

"Oh?" Aleks questioned.

The troll rubbed his broken nose, staring at the group of his friends across the way. "I want to know about Zorka's battles in Niffleheim, but if I show any interest my girlfriend will have my hide for garters."

Aleks laughed. "You'll figure something out, I'm sure. How did the fight go down between Kafirr and Jorkden?"

"Splendidly," Falkor said wolfishly. "It was brilliant and bloody. Kafirr ripped Jorkden's tail right off his backside. A battle like that only happens once in a lifetime, you know?"

The image made Aleks queasy. He bit back a burp, thumping his fist against his chest. "Maybe you should encourage Kanutte to swap the gory details with Zorka so you can hear her story."

"Oh, I like that," said Falkor, nearly toppling Aleks by a sharp slap to the back. "You're pretty smart. I'm going to find her right now."

Aleks didn't have a chance to say goodbye to the Bow-Legged Nose Basher as Henrik took his place. A trio of ellefolken girls giggled nearby, watching and hoping for an opening to greet the Stag Lord. Henrik stared at him contemplatively.

"How're you feeling?" he asked. "Ready to do this ruling business?"

"I feel great," said Aleks. "I think this will work."

"With you, it will," Henrik agreed. "Are you ready to return time to normal?"

"Tonight," he said. "When everyone's gone home."

They watched as Zaria, who was now entertaining a group of children from the various realms, shot off a display of golden fireworks which glittered and glimmered, drawing gasps of delight from the crowd. Queen Helena joined in and the two put on a show. A soft look stole into Henrik's eyes and Aleks' nudged him.

"She's got a boyfriend," he reminded gently, just as Filip joined the duo, pretending to battle the various firework creatures they conjured, and egging the children to join him, which they eagerly did.

Henrik sighed. "I know. It's for the best, but sometimes I envy you. Why couldn't it be me with the magic wishing well?"

"You two are entirely too glum over here," said Christoffer, appearing with more mugs of cider. He passed them out. "Cheers, guys. We did it."

"Let's make a toast," said Aleks. "To friends!"

"To dragon slayers," added Henrik.

"To wingmen!" shouted Christoffer, clinking cups and dragging Henrik away to the bevy of elves and ellefolken nearby.

"Life is good," said Aleks to nobody in particular.

"Very good," echoed Airi, lighting on his shoulder. She nuzzled his ear, nipping affectionately.

He stroked her feathers. "Very good indeed."

Thanks for Reading

I hope you enjoyed this fast-paced conclusion to Alek Mickelsen's trilogy. If you could take two minutes to write a review at your favorite bookseller or hangout, it would be greatly appreciated. Your reviews help other readers discover the enchanting world of Norway, Zaria Fierce, Aleks Mickelsen, and their friends. A good story as I like to say is best shared!

An Invitation

Stay in touch! You can subscribe to my free author newsletter at my website. If you do, you'll learn about upcoming releases, get behind the scenes information, and more. Additionally, everyone who signs up gets a free e-book copy of *Zaria Fierce and the Enchanted Drakeland Sword.*

Go to: https://keiragillett.com/free-download/

Coming Soon:

Christoffer Johansen and the Return to Jötunheim

New and strange occurrences are afoot in Norway, and a once enemy returns seeking aid. It's up to Christoffer and his friends – magical and human alike – to get to the source and stop it. First though, they must fulfill Queen Helena's quest to restore the Drakeland Sword. It's a difficult task that involves a witch, a raven, a brownie, and a dwarf. Can they complete their task before things get worse and evil wins?

https://keiragillett.com/book/the-return/

About the Author: Keira Gillett

Keira Gillett relished the opportunity to showcase her art in this book. She received her Bachelor of Fine Arts in Drawing and Painting from the University of Florida and has been in multiple exhibitions. When she's not working, writing, or illustrating Keira Gillett loves to snuggle with her doggie, Oskar. Like Aleks, Keira wishes she could understand her pet. If only Oskar could talk like Airi! You can follow their antics on Instagram with the #oskarpie hashtag.

Find Keira at https://keiragillett.com/

About the Artist: Eoghan Kerrigan

Eoghan Kerrigan is an illustrator from Kildare, Ireland who draws primarily fantasy characters and creatures. He studied illustration in Ballyfermot College of Further Education and has produced work for various independent projects. He has two cats and a soft spot for trolls.

Find him at http://eoghankerrigan.blogspot.ie/

About the Artist: Kaitlin Statz

Kaitlin Statz grew up in many different places, but currently lives in Sarasota, FL with her partner, Travis, and their young dog, Eezo. She attended New College of Florida and the University of Oxford for a life in the sciences before returning to her true love, art. She started her work as Statz Ink in 2015 and has been creating art ever since.

Find her at http://www.statzink.com/